PEN

Pull th

R.M. Winn is one of those blokes who never caves in. No matter how serious the situation, he hauls it out front and deals with it, hard and fast, no ifs or buts. Not even a malignant brain tumour could lay him in his tracks. He is totally self-reliant, lacks reverence, doesn't yet know what 'political correctness' means, talks no bullshit – or not much – and won't listen to any, laughs at himself easily and at others more easily.

He says he attended Ipswich Grammar School, Queensland Institute of Technology and Royal Melbourne Institute of Technology, but will not agree to saying he was educated at any of them. He adds that in one or two cases he might have actually lost ground.

For thirty-five years he was a leading rural valuer and much sought after professional court witness but just as often preferred cane-cutting, chasing scrubber cattle, running brumbies, timber-getting and driving trucks around the backblocks.

He has a swag of books to his credit, including the self-published *High Tides & Hard Rides*, *When a Tree Falls* and *Behind the Bike Shed* (available from junkyard.dog@bigpond.com) and the Penguin-published *Rough Diamonds & Real Gems*, *True Grit & Dry Wit*, *Out of the Blue*, *Up A Hollow Log* and *Bury Me Vertical*.

So that's the bloke – take him or leave him, but when the going gets tough, line up beside him and you'll be right.

Pull the Other One

RIPSNORTING AUSSIE YARNS

Collected by

R.M. WINN

PENGUIN BOOKS

PENGUIN BOOKS

Published by the Penguin Group
Penguin Group (Australia)
250 Camberwell Road, Camberwell, Victoria 3124, Australia
(a division of Pearson Australia Group Pty Ltd)
Penguin Group (USA) Inc.
375 Hudson Street, New York, New York 10014, USA
Penguin Group (Canada)
90 Eglinton Avenue East, Suite 700, Toronto, Canada ON M4P 2Y3
(a division of Pearson Penguin Canada Inc.)
Penguin Books Ltd
80 Strand, London WC2R 0RL England
Penguin Ireland
25 St Stephen's Green, Dublin 2, Ireland
(a division of Penguin Books Ltd)
Penguin Books India Pvt Ltd
11 Community Centre, Panchsheel Park, New Delhi – 110 017, India
Penguin Group (NZ)
67 Apollo Drive, Rosedale, North Shore 0632, New Zealand
(a division of Pearson New Zealand Ltd)
Penguin Books (South Africa) (Pty) Ltd
24 Sturdee Avenue, Rosebank, Johannesburg 2196, South Africa

Penguin Books Ltd, Registered Offices: 80 Strand, London, WC2R 0RL England
First published by Penguin Group (Australia), 2011

1 3 5 7 9 10 8 6 4 2

Text copyright © Ryle Winn 2011
Illustrations copyright © Mac Vines 2011

Cover and text design by Cathy Larsen © Penguin Group (Australia)
Cover photos: Blokes by Bill Bachman; tin fence, Shutterstock
Typeset in 11/17pt Sabon Roman by Cathy Larsen, Penguin Group (Australia)
Printed and bound in Australia by McPherson's Printing Group, Maryborough, Victoria

National Library of Australia
Cataloguing-in-Publication data:

Winn, Ryle, 1949–
Pull the other one : ripsnorting Aussie yarns / R. M. Winn.
9780143206057 (pbk.)
Short stories, Australian.
Australian wit and humor.
Humorous stories, Australian.

A820.8

penguin.com.au

Contents

Foreword

There is no such animal as a typical Aussie. A toothless old geezer popping up out of a mineshaft is no more typical than an orchestra conductor at the Opera House, as is everybody in between. They can be found in all walks of life. Brilliance with words – or lack of them – understatement and exaggeration are their trademarks. Laconic observations, irreverence and political incorrectness rank up there too.

A truck driver I know was being interviewed by a reporter who suggested that he was a man of few words. Know what the truckie said in reply? Nothing! He just nodded. He wasn't being a smartarse; he was simply agreeing.

Or there's my old man, who when he was asked if he'd lived in the district his whole life, had answered, 'Not yet.'

Or one mate telling his offsider 'not to get his jockstrap in a figure-eight' as the latter was freed from an unravelled roll of barbed wire – while being attacked by wasps.

Or a mate of mine who after I'd told him I was so hungry I could eat a warthog between two cot mattresses, responded with, 'That's not friggin' hungry. When you can eat an angry Tasmanian Devil between two slabs of prickly pear, that's hungry.' These are all quintessential Aussies.

This little book is a composition of humorous Australiana. In it there is a bit of everything. There are *jokes*, where the focus is on the teller – the life of the party. There are *short pub yarns*, which are typically delivered to just one or two mates by a quiet bloke in the corner, with the focus on the scene, not the teller. And finally, the *fair-dinkum yarn*, which might take a long while.

So here you have a glimpse of a motley mob that simply refuses to take itself too seriously – until the going gets real rough. Then it's a different story.

So, what's my part in it all? I've experienced an adventurous life in vocations many and varied. Take, for example, a railway sleeper-cutter, cane cutter, tobacco picker, barman, scrub cattle and brumby runner (more like 'chaser'), truckie, small farmer, builder, fertiliser agent – and then some. I've met a lot people along the way, and they've all got a yarn to tell.

I know there are a lot of louts out there looking for a laugh. I might be one myself.

Clinical trials prove that laughter adds two years and four months to your life. So, read this and let me know if it works.

Your mate,
Ryle

A Hard Day's Work

*'Mum said she wanted to shift
house one day. Let's give her
a surprise, kids!'*

Bandi-bandi snake

'This stuff tastes like piss, mate. I'd give a hundred bucks for a case of good old Queensland Fourex.'

'Fourex is not much better than what you've got in front of you. Slab of VB would do me.'

Arnie and Ralph were nearly skint. Only fifty bucks between them. Nowhere to sleep. If they bought tucker, they'd have nothing left for more grog.

'Seriously, mate. If we can't find another job we're stuffed.'

'Fret not, my intrepid explorer mate. Something always bobs up. Always has before,' Arnie reckoned. He was the optimist . . .

'So, what's for tea?'

'Get pissed and forget about it.'

They'd got the arse from an oil rig in Sumatra for retailing a little mood-lifter on the side, and were making their way down to Bali. From there, they figured it couldn't be too hard to get home to Oz. It'd been hot and slow-going, but the future was still looking rosy enough – until they reached Bandar Lampung, where three men bailed them up for Arnie's back pack.

'Follow that bastard, Arnie, and get your bag back. I'll fix the other two.'

The decoy led Arnie down an alley – the oldest trick in the book. It was ten minutes before Arnie staggered back to the main street, empty-handed and breathing hard... but the thieves had done their work. Ralph had been going okay till reinforcements overpowered him. Wallet, passport, the last of the cash – all gone.

They were drowning their sorrows in a seedy bar, drinking the stray coins left in their pockets, when a low voice interrupted them.

'You look for work? Plenty cash. I pay straightaway. American dollar.'

'See, always happens. Just when you need it most, eh, Ralphy boy? What's the job, mate?'

'First we have drink. I pay. Then we talk.'

'Suits me.'

'Me, too,' Ralph chimed in.

Custom satisfied, the trio got down to business.

'I have export pizness. Very good money. Need good Aussie workers.'

'You got the right blokes. When can we start?' Arnie asked.

'Tomorrow. I meet you here eight o'clock.'

'What do we need?'

'I give everything. Experience, training, all equipment.'

Next morning.

'Here. We start here.'

'For fuck's sake, mate, we're 20 kilometres in the bush. What the hell is this job?'

'Very good money. You catch for me black-and-yellow bandi-bandi snake. Very hard to catch. Thousand dollar. Two thousand very big one.' He stretched his arms full width. 'You take snake by tail with one hand and hold on. Use other hand and slide up long way to top and clamp on snake head. Put him in bag. Very easy. Here you bag. Pick up four o'clock.' Then he was gone so fast neither Arnie nor Ralph had the chance to say a word.

'Beggars can't be choosers, mate. Caught many snakes?'

'Nope. Looks like we're about to learn.'

Four o'clock.

As promised, their employer arrived, on time and for shit's sake driving a gold Mercedes.

'You not look good. You have been in big fight. How many snake?'

'None.'

'You pizz off, then. You not work for me.'

With that, he sped off, leaving them there.

'Arsehole,' Ralph yelled, shaking his fist after the cloud of dust, with the arm of his torn shirt flapping and the other hand holding up his pants. 'Wonder if we can hitch a lift out of here?'

One driver passed them, slowed down, stared, nearly veered off the road and kept driving. The second car to happen by them was driven by an Aussie.

'Jesus Christ, what happened to you blokes? Shit, you both look like you've been through a chaffcutter.'

'Well, we were supposed to be catching snakes for some rip-off dickhead, but Ralph got it a bit wrong.'

'Huh, not the black-and-yellow bandi-bandi? Worth a million bucks but you'll go straight to jail if you're caught with one. Never heard of anyone being mauled by one, though. Actually, they're constrictors. Don't bite. So, how'd you get so messed up?'

'Well, me and Ralphy here staggered around the bush most of the day, wondering if the bandi-bandi even existed. Then, just as we were about to give it away, I spotted one lying there, quiet. I figured it must have nodded off. About a metre of it was sticking out of the bushes. *Bloody beauty*, I thought, *a big bugger* too.

'I took the bastard by the tail, and Ralphy ran his hand right up along the snake's body and into the bushes, getting ready to clamp its jaw shut. Was going all right too, until he jammed his thumb fair up the arse of a tiger.'

———

Take the bait

'Have a look at these, Igor,' Dave said to his mate and part-time employee, as he ran his hand over a rack of fishing lures. 'New stock. Bloody beauties, eh?'

Dave owned and ran the best camping, fishing and bait shop in the business. The place was always busy. He made up fishing rods to order, had his own brand of lures, rigged up tackle for all types of fishing, bought in bulk and passed on the savings to his customers. Dave even had his own half-hour Saturday-morning talk show and a column in the *Fishing and Camping News*.

No flies on Dave. Funny how he seemed not to notice he was almost blind. Granted, his wife worked half days with him Monday to Wednesday, and Igor got in the way on Saturdays. Otherwise he was on his own.

Saturday afternoons were bedlam. The place was always jam-packed. This particular weekend was no different.

'Shit, mate, how many of these bloody things did you buy?' Igor asked, placing another six fishing rods on the rack down the back.

'Three hundred . . . and I've sold sixty during the week. Nice little kids rods. Good for the boat too, eh? What colour is that boxful?'

Dave left Igor to do the unpacking and went to the front of the shop to attend to the counter.

Running his hand the full length of the rod and feeling the size and shape of a box the customer placed on the counter, Dave said, 'Little four-inch Alvey, eh? Like your choice. Good combination. Sixty bucks all up.'

He turned to the next person in the queue.

'Yeah, those little tents are good value for the kids,' Dave said, after he'd felt the box and picked it up to feel the weight of it. 'They'll have a lot of fun in it. How the bloody hell they make them for that price I don't know. That's the go these days. Everything made in China.'

As he closed the till, a big tradesman type, displaying ample bum crack, walked into the store and spoke to Dave briefly.

'Right down the second aisle, mate, on the left,'

Dave said in response. 'You'll find a fellow unpacking some more boxes of them. Walking off the shelves, they are. Good value. Twenty-five bucks. Don't get that sort of deal often.'

'No. I read about them in your column. That's why I'm here.'

The tradesman lumbered off. He was only away from the counter a few minutes before he returned with the rod. Waiting in line, he fished about in his pocket for his wallet. As he withdrew it, it slipped from his grasp and fell to the floor. Stepping back a pace, he bent over to retrieve it and as he did so, dropped a fart that thickened the air and smelt like a cross between a sulphur pit and a pig pen. The accompanying noise was similar to the intermittent burble of a hard-to-start two-stroke motor.

Some customers looked appalled. Others pretended it hadn't happened. But nobody made any comment.

After the tradesman had put his purchase on the counter, he tendered two twenty-dollar notes and waited for Dave to give him his change. When none was forthcoming, he challenged Dave.

'What's this gimmick? I gave you $40. Not in the habit of being taken down.'

'Gimmick? What do you mean? No, mate. That's

right. Twenty-five bucks for the rod, and another fifteen for the duck caller and the mullet gut.'

———

Eskimo Joe

Tradesmen all suffer from the same syndrome. It's called the 'factor four' disease. If they are supposed to arrive at eight o'clock, they arrive at midday. If 'any time Monday' is specified, they will arrive on Thursday. If September is the appointed month then they will arrive in December – which is bloody freezing in the north of Canada where Eskimos live – and for this reason Eskimo Joe was not at all popular.

Eskimo Joe was a contract igloo builder and he was in the shit because he was late, like late in the middle of winter. His chainsaw had broken down. He had three igloos to build and he felt pressured because his clients were living in a ghetto of busted arse, last year's model igloos that had been half thawed and refrozen. Hardly good enough to weather the usual sixty to eighty blizzards you'd expect during the season.

So Joe had to get his arse into gear. However there was a further hitch. Because of the crook weather the Tundra Shire Council had run into trouble too. The new subdivision hadn't been finished – in fact it hadn't been started.

So the only options left for Joe's clients were to buy remnant allotments from a previous subdivision, which all faced north. Not good. Aspect was everything. Facing the tundra would allow the blizzards to blow fair up their air tunnels.

Still, better than nothing, the owners, Icicle Bill, Husky Jane and Syd Skidoo concurred, so Joe mushed up his gang and ripped into the job. There was a bit of competition among the three clients for the miserable allotments, and it was thought that the fairest method of allocation would be to draw straws. But gallantry prevailed and the men allowed Husky to have her choice first. It wouldn't do to fall foul of Husky – she could knock up a breakfast of seal strips and penguin eggs like nobody else, and other offerings were sometimes dispensed with good grace also.

Of course, Husky chose the site that allowed her igloo to face north-north-west instead of due north. The other two blocks were identical, both facing due north, and so there shouldn't have been trouble choosing, except that Bill wanted to live beside Husky. To reinforce his preference he cracked Syd over the earmuff with a reindeer horn and knocked him on his arse. Arrangements concluded.

Soon enough the igloos were completed and the transactions for payment in polar-bear skins satisfactorily receipted.

It was only a fortnight later, at Husky's housewarming, that the conversation turned to temperature. As foreshadowed the igloos were less than optimum in terms of climate control.

Husky told the men that her new home was so cold that if she slept on her side her bottommost nipple nearly froze. In fact she'd already had a couple of doses of frostbite so she had to alternate sides during the night. But one morning last week she woke to find she'd slept face down. Bloody hell, she was nearly stuck to the floor.

Icicle Bill was quiet for a while before he spoke. 'That's nothing,' he squeaked.

Husky and Skidoo spun around in alarm to face their mate. 'Shit, Bill, what happened to your voice?'

He answered, 'That igloo of mine would freeze the walls off a grass humpy. When my balls stop clattering about and thaw out, I'll be able to talk properly, I hope. Curse that blizzard last night. I reckon my igloo is the coldest of them all.'

'Bullshit. I know without doubt that mine's coldest,' Skiddy said. 'Have a look at this.'

Without more ado, he dropped his fur dacks and pulled down his arctic fox jocks. Then he tore off a frozen skid mark, leant over to the slush lamp, and held it over the flame. After only a few seconds it fizzed and sputtered, then ignited as a loud *faarrrttt!* erupted and blew out the lamp.

———

In the trade

Young Conor had finished school a year ago but so far hadn't landed a job. He'd applied for dozens of apprenticeships: electrician, plumber, stripper (round-one interview only), carpenter, frig mechanic, barman, lapdancer (wrong sex), plasterer, painter, pole dancer (still waiting for reply from the electric light company).

Nope, nothing. He was getting quite despondent, but through sheer persistence Conor finally landed a job as an offsider to a handyman – not exactly an apprenticeship but who knew where it might lead. While the lad was keen he was as dumb as dog shit.

'Sonny,' said the boss, laughing, 'duck down to the hardware store and buy me a new bubble for me spirit level.'

In due course Conor arrived back. 'Here you are,

boss,' he said, holding out a drinking straw with his thumbs over the ends. 'The hardware man said he didn't sell them singly and he'd bill you out for a dozen.'

Poor Conor.

'Me boy, go and buy me a left-handed screwdriver,' the boss requested the next day, and the lad was away for all of his smoko.

'Conor,' the boss said one day as they pulled up outside the hardware shop, 'hop in and collect those two-by-fours I ordered last week.'

The lad arrived back saying that the order had been misplaced and the bloke who took it was away sick.

'Well, go back and tell them to make a new order up while we wait.'

Conor set off again but was away for only a minute.

'Boss, they don't stock anything like two-by-fours. The casual wants to know if something else might do.'

'Jesus Christ. Ask him about four-by-twos. Have they got any of them?'

Off Conor went again.

'Yes, they have,' he said when he returned.

'Well . . . ?' the boss said.

'Well, what?'

'For Christ's sake, lad. They're the same bloody thing.'

'Oh!' . . . and off he went again.

As expected, he was back soon after. He was getting to know the way quite well.

'He wants to know how long you want them.'

The boss couldn't believe his ears and sat shaking his head. 'I must be surrounded by idiots.' Then he added, 'Tell him a fuckin' long time. We're building a shed.'

———

Pointy end

Santa had had a gutful. Right through autumn and into early winter he'd been mustering and breaking in the reindeer on his own. All his usual contract musterers had pissed off to other jobs that were paying better money. Some went fishing. Others took off to ski in Aspen. More still went building igloos on spec. No two ways about it, this year Santa had to be his own cowboy – or doe boy, stag boy . . . whatever. He had to do it all himself anyway.

Just a month out from Christmas, Donner and Blitzen had become a worry too. Donner needed treatment for an ingrown ~~toenail~~ hoof and Blitzen had developed chilblains that threatened to freeze up to become frostbite and turn gangrenous. What *friggin'* next? Santa thought, and then he found out. . . the vet's bill, that's what. Nothing else for it; he had to extend the overdraft – but not before the hassle of having to threaten to melt the ensuite off the manager's igloo with his oxy bottle.

And it wasn't over. Of late, Santa's memory had been letting him down. Last year his sleigh had been substantially damaged and Santa had parked it in the hangar with good intentions to have it fixed. Only now, when he'd reversed it out to give it a grease and oil change, did he remember. He shuddered as he recalled his final drop-off last year. When he'd called to Rudolph to land on the Schmitt house, the idiot must have had an earful of snow because he'd misinterpreted the order and landed on the roof of the dunny.

With a bit of luck, Santa might still be able to have the sleigh repaired just in time for Christmas. In a panic he sent it off to the Midnight Sun Paint and Panel shop, pleading with them to prioritise his job.

After he got the sleigh back and things were quiet for a few days, Santa breathed a sigh of relief. Maybe the jinx had been lifted, run its course. Perhaps the tide of his fortunes had turned.

But then on Friday night a fax came through from the Tundra Produce Agency with a terse message: 'Your late order for reindeer rations will be given immediate attention, but for the extra service a 20 per cent surcharge will apply. Please advise.'

'Bullshit!' Santa yelled, scaring the arses off a couple of nearby elves doing overtime in the workshop. Two others down the far end looked at each other with raised eyebrows.

'The bastards only charge like wounded polar bears because they've got us over a barrel. Next year I'll fence off a thousand acres and grow a patch of moss and lichens myself. At this rate, the feed bill for Rudolph, Randolph and the gang will bleed me dry.'

He checked his bank statement and realised he was overdrawn. On ringing the bank, he was told that his credit had been cut off and he should go to see their subsidiary finance company, Arctic Shafters.

Poor old Santa. If it wasn't one thing, it was another. Surely nothing else could go wrong? He was convinced his ulcer would start playing up or he'd come out in a nasty nervous rash.

It was more than a nervous rash that broke out when he was informed that the Frigid Workers Union had called for a series of rolling strikes, demanding pay increases, improved penalty rates and new-season woolly earmuffs for both elves and chimney sweeps.

Fuming with rage, Santa went outside and screamed, 'For Christ's sake! What the fuck else can go wrong?' and startled his reindeer herd into a stampede.

A black mood settled over Santa. It got blacker next morning when he discovered that Rudolph had severe colic and the vet had to be summoned once again, at pace.

After smoko, Santa was sitting with his head in his hands bemoaning his fate and settling into deep dark depression when he heard the sweet voice of an angel coming along the passageway.

'Season's greetings, Santa. Where do you want this pine tree?'

And that's why the Christmas angel always sits on the very top of the Christmas tree.

———

Oonga Boonga

In the days before modern technology, aerial navigation was all done by the human eye. But in New Guinea the constant low-level cloud tested even the stout-hearted. Tree-top-level navigation using jungle tracks and flowering vines as aids was standard. To compound the problems airstrips were often half the normal length.

In 1972, as Gough Whitlam, six reporters, twelve advisors and two makeup girls took off from Cairns airport, the Cessna was overloaded, and the pilot hadn't even climbed aboard. Now realising what lay ahead of them, even before they'd gained enough altitude to clear the Atherton Tablelands they had to jettison two journos, three advisors, all the parachutes and the girls' mascara.

Now they were in business. Destination New Guinea.

First things first. The boss advisor told the second advisor to ask a reporter to consult a makeup girl to find out where they were going, and on being informed wanted to know what the hell they were going to do there. He then explained to Gough that they would touch down at Mt Hagen about midday in time to open the local show, where he would also be required to judge the hairstyles of the young fellows. As there were whispers about gaining independence within a couple of years and underlying currents of unrest, Gough was advised that he should maximise the opportunities to show what a great man he was, and the hairstyle comp was really a crock of shit anyway.

A low-level dummy pass over what looked like the Mt Hagen township scattered a mob of cattle eating metre-high kunai grass off the airstrip, sending them in all directions. The approach had been a tad low even for the experienced pilot, and he was concerned one or more of the exuberant tribesmen's spear tips had punctured a wheel or two and he had no jack. So be it – he was committed.

In due course Gough and his entourage were welcomed in fine style and after lunch of wild boar with a side salad of yams, Gough got right into the personal promotions business.

'During the next three years, I will build for you an international airport here to replace the 600-metre runway.'

'Oonga boonga!' yelled the tribesmen and women as they waved their spears.

'I will introduce paid maternity leave.'

'Oonga boonga!' went up the chant, accompanied by the stamping of feet in the ankle-deep mud.

The journos were having an easy time of it since all they had to do was write 'oonga boonga' on their clipboards and simply added multiplication signs alongside. That would do for copy to send home.

Gough turned to the entourage. 'Fellas, what do you reckon? Going pretty well, eh? These tribesmen are mighty enthusiastic. They love me. I'll keep going.'

'I'll have a computer and broadband in every hut,'

he added with a sweep of his arm.

'Oonga boonga! Oonga boonga!' More spear waving and rattling.

Gough bent down and whispered into the ear of one of the makeup girls, 'I like the sound of "Oonga boonga". It says a lot without saying anything.'

Still he went on. 'I will build a new bitumen road to Port Moresby so that you can go down to the movies or the disco on Saturday nights.'

'Oonga boonga!' The crowd closed in and the spear rattling became more intense.

Finally the address was over and Gough smiled broadly as he folded his notes. After chewing some betel nut with the council of chiefs, he was ushered back towards the Cessna. The mob of cattle was no longer on the runway, the pilot was pleased to note. They were now resting in the shade of a grass hut that doubled as an air-traffic control tower.

Just as Gough was about step onto the ladder leading up to the plane, the chairman chief grabbed his shoulder and said quietly, 'If I was you, I'd watch where I was putting my feet. Wouldn't want to tramp in all that oonga boonga before you get back in the plane, would you?'

———

Teamwork

Wazza was a bloody good mechanic in the specialised workshop of Mercedes Benz. He was highly regarded by all: fast, accurate, and deadly at changing tyres in a few seconds. His mechanical diagnoses were quick and seldom wrong. He worked well under pressure too, which was why the big jobs were always assigned to him.

Today the pride of the fleet – the big Merc, a showpiece from the factory of Benz, albeit not a new vehicle – was to be used as a wedding car for the Mayor's daughter's ceremony at 2 p.m. What an opportunity for advertising, but everything had to be spot on. Wazza was allocated two apprentices to help with the task, and given the instructions to boot them up the arse if they didn't perform.

'Righto, you blokes,' Wazza said with authority, 'now that I've done the service, I want this car detailed to a standard never before achieved, y'hear? Now get into it.'

Well, talk about performing. Those kids were a credit to whoever chose them from the hundred applicants. They washed, vacuumed, polished and did anything else they could think of. The white-wall tyres were painted. The spats sparkled. The nickel-plated, high-tensile, coil-spring sidewinders gleamed. The sun visor was tightened. Door handles were treated with degreaser. Wow! The kids were sure they would be recommended for promotion.

All Wazza had left to do was test-drive the chariot, come back to the workshop, tighten the wheel nuts and enter the service in the log book. He simply thrived on challenges such as these. He would then give it a final dust off and buff up and leave it out front for collection by the groom's best man, all with half an hour to spare by his reckoning.

Through the built-up areas Wazza drove, enjoying the luxury of being behind the wheel of such a classy machine. As the countryside opened up, Wazza took the Merc up to 200kph and it felt like 80kph. It swept around corners with no sign of drift, then straightened out and sat on the road solid as a rock. He hit the brakes and the ABS cut in beautifully. Wazza was in awe: *what a bloody machine*. Fully satisfied, and with an inner glow, he turned the big saloon for home and planted the foot.

If Wazza hadn't been doing 250kph, he probably would have had time to focus on whatever it was lying on the bitumen. As it was he had no hope. The sounds of tyre blowouts sent a shiver through him. *Jesus Christ*, he thought. A sheet of Weldmesh with the ends turned up had apparently fallen off a truck. Not one puncture… two, on the driver's side. Now he was in strife.

Wazza being Wazza, he got his brain properly into gear and ripped his mobile phone out of his pocket with one hand as he turned the wrist of the other to check the time.

He spoke quickly to the older apprentice. 'Load the compressor and generator onto the truck. Get a couple of tyres off the rack and two new tubes. What? No, you dickhead. The next rack. The ones you must be looking at are for the council grader. Then get your arse out here.'

'Out where?'

'Twenty kilometres on the north coast road.'

'Okay, be there in ten,' the apprentice answered.

Wazza pocketed his phone, checked his watch again and did what his training dictated. There was no time to spare. Frantically he loosened the wheel nuts a fraction, then jacked up the first wheel, found a couple of rocks, blocked up the hub and took that wheel off. Then he jacked up the second wheel and was just loosening the nuts when a strange ute came to a sliding halt beside him.

Nice of him to offer assistance, Wazza thought.

Out hopped a mountain of a swarthy bloke, brandishing a baseball bat. He went around to the front of the Merc and started bashing the windscreen in.

'Jesus!' screamed Wazza. 'What the fuck do you think you're doing?'

'Hey, bro, if you're taking the wheels, I'm knocking off the stereo.'

———

Hang on there!

Sean, Pat and Mick hadn't had easy lives, not till this point anyway. Sean, the poor bugger, had pinched an apple and got seven years transportation to Van Diemen's Land for his indiscretion. He said that if he'd known Tasmania was full of apples he'd have pinched an orange for a bit of variety.

And Pat, well, he copped his sentence because he stole a bag of hops to make some homebrew and got seven years for that. If he'd known Tassie was Australia's hop-growing state, he'd have pinched a bottle of Irish Cream Whisky for variety too.

Mick got seven years when he was caught having it off with the local magistrate's wife. He told the court that she wasn't as good in bed as his own wife, and his sentence was increased to fourteen years. He thought that was a little unfair since the magistrate was having it off with Mick's wife at the same time and obviously getting the better end of the deal.

Be all that as it may, the felons had become mates while incarcerated. In idle moments they fantasised about escaping. They hit on the idea of pinching the commandant's three-metre punt and sailing the 17000 kilometres home, a plan that they acted on. They were discovered three kilometres out to sea, with Sean holding his shirt up to catch the breeze while the others paddled – Mick with a cake-tin lid and Pat with a dried Tasmanian devil skin.

For this misdemeanour, they were each given 200 lashes at the triangle and sentenced to hang on Friday morning. A public holiday was declared and the townspeople alerted to the forthcoming gala event.

As there were no qualified tradesmen holding Union tickets in the settlement, the trio had to erect their own scaffold. Being reasonable handymen they made a fair job of it and then calculated the drop, their own weights and the lengths of rope needed for a clean, neck-snapping death. At the end of the project they were well pleased with the result.

Come Friday morning they were fair shitting themselves but there was no time for further pleas for clemency. All was set to go.

As Sean was led up the step he looked resolute and, once there, was asked if he had any last words.

'No, sir.'

No time was wasted in putting the bag over his head and dropping the floor out from under him.

But instead of tightening under his chin, the rope knot unravelled, frayed, parted and Sean hit the ground with only a jinked neck for his trouble.

'It is the unwritten law,' the hangman said, 'we cannot make another attempt. You are pardoned – a free man.'

Sean tore off down to the pub to celebrate his good fortune.

After lengthy discussions between the hangman, the rope splicer and the knot tier the stage was set to see Mick off to his maker.

'Michael O'Flaherty, do you have any last words?'

'No, sir.'

No time was wasted preparing to send Mick off to his maker.

However the splicer and the hangman had stuffed up again, and Mick dropped lightly to the ground, a free man also. Staightaway he ripped off his hood and dashed down to the boozer to catch up with Sean.

Pat was led up to the scaffold and stood quietly, looking intently at the rope. Just before the hood was placed over his head the statutory question was asked of him. 'Patrick McGee, do you have any last words?'

'Yeah, I think I can see what's wrong with that knot.'

————

'If he's not the road tester for Michelin tyres, I'll throw the book at him.'

Your Shout

'Bubby, if you've just done what I think you have, we'd better get out of here.'

Dave's long drop

Dad and Dave were having a quiet beer at the local pub. Actually, Dad was having a quiet beer, but Dave, who'd never had a drink in a proper hotel with his father before, was getting rather carried away.

'Steady up a bit, son,' Dad cautioned. 'Beer is for drinking, not guzzling. You'll be drunk before three o'clock. Mum will feed the chooks and milk the cow, so take your time; there's no rush.'

Ignoring Dad's warning, Dave ripped into the grog. Of course, it wasn't long before he was more than a bit fuzzy.

'Didn't know you had a brother, Dad. As a matter fact, he looks a lot like you,' Dave said, trying to focus.

'Boy, if you were a rope, you'd have one frayed end. You'd better settle back a bit. Go and sit on the verandah.'

'Where's the long drop first, Pa? One of those new-fangled shitcans you told me about with the water flush? I need an urgent visit.'

Obviously, Dave's digestive system was being given a workout. 'Caught short' might have described his condition.

'Out this door,' Dad nodded, 'along the verandah,'

he pointed around the corner, 'down three steps,' he indicated down, 'turn right,' he held out his arm, 'first on the left.'

Dave took off at pace, left hand clamped tightly on the seat of his trousers.

Dad drank three schooners of beer, smoked two roll-yer-owns and kicked a dog out of the way before he started to worry about his wayward son.

Just as he'd decided to mount a search party, Dad saw Dave stagger in, doubled over and obviously in pain.

'Strike trouble, son? What's wrong? You got a guts-ache?'

'You should have warned me, Pa,' Dave complained, 'I ain't using those new dunnies again. They're danger-ous.'

'What are you talking about, boy? Where have you been?'

'Well, I went out the door, along the verandah, around the corner, down the steps, turned right, second on the left.'

'First on the left,' Dad corrected.

'Second,' Dave argued. 'I found the place all right.'

Dad frowned. 'Nope. Don't know where you were, but the dunny is exactly where I said it was.'

'Well, there was a dunny in this room too, but I must admit,' Dave said, starting to straighten up, 'I wasn't all that gone on it. Every time I tried use the foot flusher and get up off the seat, it grabbed me by the balls and wouldn't let go till I sat down again.'

'Dave, you dimwit, you must have been in the laundry, sitting on the mop bucket.'

———

The worst sound

Winston, Jock and Blue were in Melbourne, sitting in the Young & Jackson Hotel, the pub on Flinders Street, getting pissed and trying to think straight while gazing at the portrait of Chloe, in all her nude glory, hanging on the wall behind the bar.

'If she was my missus, when I'd get home the second bang would be the sound of the front door closing,' Blue said, draining his pot.

'Aye, she's a bonnie lassie, all right,' agreed Jock. 'Speaking of bangs, what's the worst noise you've ever heard in your life?'

Winston answered. 'Definitely during the war while we were being shelled from across the Channel. It was pretty bad one night in particular.'

The others were all ears.

'Yes, indeed. That evening a shell exploded right in the doorway of our air-raid shelter.'

'Would've been a hell of a noise,' Blue commented. 'Don't you reckon, Jock?'

Jock nodded but looked only slightly impressed.

Winston continued. 'But that's not the end of it. The sound of the shell exploding was nothing much. The worst noise I ever heard was my bangers and mash slopping onto the floor.'

Jock took up the story. 'I nearly copped a stray bullet in Korea. It came from a sniper above, glanced off my helmet, knocked off my glasses, skinned my knuckles . . .'

Here, Jock paused to study his whisky, and Winston commented, 'The noise of that bullet hitting your helmet would've rattled you, would it not, my Scottish friend?'

Jock nodded. 'Things got worse, though. The bullet blew a hole in my bagpipes while I was playing the last few bars of "Donald, Where's Your Troosers?" Aye, a sad, haunting sound it was, what with Donald choking down into a heap and squeaking his last notes. That was the worst sound I ever heard.'

Obviously still focusing on Chloe, Blue after careful

deliberation said, 'Beautiful piece of work, that sheila.'

The pros and cons of a night in bed with the subject of the portrait seemed foremost in Blue's mind. The topic of the worst noises the mates had ever heard seemed to be trailing second, until he added, 'Yes, she's nearly as good-looking as a sheila I had myself, once. Reminds me of the worst noise I ever heard.'

Two pairs of eyes swung to him.

'Bit of a sad end. Didn't even get to say goodbye.'

'Well?' Winston asked impatiently.

'Well, you see, her old man used to work the night shift and I'd visit her often – satisfy her needs, like. I was in bed with her one night when the bastard came home early, and we heard him coming up the steps. I scrambled into the wardrobe starkers, breathing hard, and he must have heard me. Bit of an ugly scene, I can tell you. Anyway, I went to jump out the window, and I'd nearly cleared the sill when the mongrel caught me one-handed by the nuts and hung on. The worst sound I ever heard was the sound of that hairy gorilla opening his pocketknife with his teeth.'

———

Cocktail hour

Sam, short for 'sample bag' (full of shit and you've got to carry him all day), and Ocker were all cashed up and looking for adventure. They were making their way down from the Northern Territory. They'd never been any further south than Katherine before.

Ockie had seen a job advertisement in the Melbourne *Age* and confided to Sam. 'Mate, what do you make of this?' he said, handing the newspaper to him.

'Mmm,' said Sam, 'Hmm.'

'Hmm, what?'

'Mmm, I don't know what to make of it. It says there's only one position available.'

'We could share the job. Might be better that way anyway. Give a bloke a bit of a break.'

'Let me read it right through,' said Sam.

'During spring we have twelve new fillies that need servicing. Will be pregnancy tested progressively. Only top studs will be considered. Apply with CV in hand. Flemington Racecourse.'

'Sounds too good to be true, mate. Better book a train ticket from Oodnadatta as soon as we can. Might need a new pair of double pluggers and a couple of singlets too. They say it gets cold down there.'

In due course, on Tuesday, 2 November, the pair arrived on the racecourse and by a stroke of luck there was a bit of a bush race meeting in progress. Actually there were hundreds of pisspots staggering about the car park trying to find their cars. It appeared they must have got pissed pretty quick or there had been a meeting the day before too. Perhaps they weren't game to leave the grounds in case they were breath-tested. Lucky they brought their tucker boxes.

'Jesus Christ,' Ockie said. 'Bloody hell.'

'Christ almighty,' Sam observed, 'Bleedin' hades.'

As the mates entered a big white circus tent they were flabbergasted again.

'Friggin' hell, mate,' Ockie gasped.

'My oath,' Sam added. 'Look at all these fillies. I wonder which twelve they meant. We'll have to ask about a bit. Be a bugger if we got the wrong ones.'

But all afternoon the mates drew blanks. On enquiring of dozens upon dozens of likely lassies if they would like servicing till they dropped down pregnant, the result was always the same, 'Get fucked, losers. Go and root each other.' Some of the other suggestions were less polite.

It was disconcerting to the Territorians until they

found themselves at cocktail hour in the Members' bar.

'This is a bit of a break, mate,' Sam said. 'There're five or half a dozen fillies over by the bar. Let's try our luck.'

Ockie took the lead. 'Er, girls, would you like us to buy you a drink?'

'Why not?' said one, being supported by a friend.

'Yeah, why not?' said another, unable to stand.

'What would you like?' Sam intervened, glancing at the drinks list and blushing, then at the prices and nearly fainting.

'I'll have two Slippery Nipples,' she said, getting the okay from her friend.

Said another, 'A Screw on the Wall for me and my partner.'

'Just a Naked Waiter for me,' said the last.

Trying to act sophisticated, Sam enquired of his territory mate, 'Of what might you like imbibe?'

'The special, my friend, the Horse's Head. I think it will be worth it at the end of the day.'

'Jesus, mate,' Sam said, emptying out his wallet. 'I'd better have a Horse's Arse myself. I don't want them killing two horses.'

———

Brotherly love

Every afternoon Dinny fronted up to the bar at
O'Flaherty's and had a pint of Guinness on his way
home after work. For years he had maintained the
habit. Mick the barman could set his clock by him.

He was a quiet man, was Dinny. Thoughtful, by
appearance anyway, or maybe just thick, but a quiet
man all the same.

'Ye'll be having the same as always, Dinny, I expect?'

It was a question that needed no answer since the
Guinness had already been poured and settled nicely.

'Yes, I need the pint for meself, but today I'll also
need another for me brother who's gone away.'

'Oh. Gone away . . . like you mean to the other side?'
Mick said in a sombre tone as he drew the pint.

'To be sure. He's crossed to the other side.'

'Ah, that's the way of it. A good man I'll be thinking,
was he?'

'Yes, I'll be missing him,' Dinny added.

However, to the barman's bewilderment Dinny
didn't drink the spare pint but left it sitting on the bar,
as if his brother might drop in for it.

The following afternoon the same charade took

place. Mick didn't say anything, figuring that the grief would pass in time. He also calculated that if he waited till Dinny took his leave, he could sell the pint a second time.

Week after week, month after month, each afternoon the barman poured two drinks for Dinny as the mourning went on. Then one day Dinny called and ordered one pint only.

Ah, at last, Mick thought, *Dinny's through the worst of it.* That grief is a terrible thing, to be sure, but there's nought for it except time.

'Feeling a little better, Dinny, me mate?' Mick asked as he set down the Guinness. 'The head coming a little clearer and the soul a little easier then.'

'You're a good man, Mick, but I don't know what you're meaning.'

'I'm meaning the single pint, me mate. Come to terms with your brother's passing at last, have you?'

'Passing? What makes you think that? Callum crossed over the Channel to England six months ago for a well-paid labouring job. No, the pint's for him as always. Me, I've given up drinking meself.'

———

Who needs it?

'So, how are you getting along with the missus these days?' Jock asked Murphy as he placed a pint of Guinness in front of him, and then slid a tankard of Newcastle Brown across the table to their mate Taffy. Then Jock retraced six steps to the bar, and picked up a double whisky, counted his change a few times, then sat down again.

'Don't talk to her much these days, the silly bloody woman,' Murphy answered. 'Since the kids have gone she threatens to leave every week. All she needs is a bit of a holiday. I told her to go to stay with her sister for a while.'

'What about you, Taffy? How's Maureen?'

'She's got no bloody brains either. As you know, she's built like a straight piece of No. 8 wire. She's that bloody skinny she has to run around under the shower to get wet. Now she's going on a diet.'

A week later, on pay day, the workmates were back at the bar of the Pig and Whistle, and the same topic arose.

'Anyway, Jock, how's your bonny wee lassie?'

'Half as big as a bus these days. Wished her brains

matched her weight. Bloody fool! Know what she went and did? She went and bought a car and neither of us has got a licence.'

Murphy took up. 'My missus is stupider than I thought. She took my advice about a bit of a holiday. I thought when she said she'd booked a cruise she meant for both of us. Nope. Just for herself. And know what I found among her luggage, which she'd spread all over the bed? A pack of thirty condoms . . . and she doesn't even have a dick.'

———

Technical knockout

It was Woolamakanka's turn to host the annual cricket match against the team from Central. Friendly rivalry had been the way since day one. In recent years Woola's line-up had boasted a middle order that was starting to rise to the challenge. But Woola's tailenders were the problem as usual, according to Chook.

Numbers had been short, and so the eleventh man was the local chess champion with his Coke-bottle glasses. However, Central, from 200 kilometres down the line, had one good bowler now and two batsmen who could connect at least every second ball, so the trophy was coveted and competition was fierce.

Against the odds, Saturday's play turned out to be most satisfactory for the Woola team. As predicted, Central's star bowler, Sizzler, took most of the wickets and one wide took out the windscreen of Chook's Land-Cruiser. Although Bishop, the chess player, slipped in a cowpat and did in his ankle, and one of the kids cut his foot on a broken stubby interrupting play for a while, Woola emerged victorious in the first innings.

Saturday night was always a big one, with both teams getting together, first at the pub and later at the motel. Tonight was about standard, with the girls getting into the swing of things too. Shazz had gone easy on the vodka but had an extra 40-oz bottle if need be. Kath called ~~R~~Mandy a hot pants and told her to keep away from Vince, who at that moment she could not see. Later she spotted him doing up his fly, but gave him the benefit of the doubt.

The pub closed while the night was still a pup . . . but the bottle-o stayed open.

Back at the motel Ferret told Bazza to steady up on the piss or they'd run out and Bazza gave him a belt in the mouth and copped a beauty back. Toolie tried to intervene, and Shazz yelled to keep out of it or she'd give him one herself. Of course Jimmy had to start mouthing off and Kevin put him in a headlock to settle him down but it seemed to have the opposite effect.

Then the piss did run out – shock, horror.

'Orright, youse lot. Who's going to get the pizzas and the Chinese? How about you girls do that and us blokes will go and get some more booze?' Sizzler suggested.

Seemed reasonable. Consensus achieved.

An hour later, after the tucker had been consumed, Chook noted, 'I thought we bought four cartons of stubbies. Where's the other one? For that matter where's Toolie? I didn't see him come back.'

'He reckoned he'd be a while. He was chatting up the sheila at the drive-through,' Ferret informed them. 'He had a carton of piss on his shoulder.'

So the search was on for Toolie. Hither and thither they looked: up and down the street . . . down the lane . . . across the railway line. No go. Finally they had to give up. It was late and they were tired. Before going upstairs, three of the blokes ducked around the corner behind the motel and, in the half dark, started to have a piss. As their eyes adjusted pretty well, almost simultaneously, they spied Toolie spreadeagled on the concrete.

'Shit, mate, what happened?' Sizzler asked Toolie, who was now sitting upright.

'You right, Toolie?'

'I was mugged.'

'Bloody looks like it,' they observed.

'Fuckin' knocked me out, the bastards. Look at me forehead,' he said, putting a hand to an egg-sized lump. 'Smashed the piss and broke the beer glasses I stole too by the looks.'

There was no doubt about that.

'Did they get your wallet?'

'Nuh,' he said, feeling his pocket.

Chook said, 'What did they get then? Why did they mug you? Wouldn't they have wanted the booze? Mate, I don't think you were mugged. I think you just fell over.'

'Bullshit. I was trying to get away and I was just about to run between those two palm trees when they jumped me and one of them hit me with a waddy.' Again he put his hand to his forehead.

'You're a dickhead, Toolie. Those palm trees are painted on the concrete block wall.'

———

Concorde

In France, 27 October 1975 was slated for the biggest event in the history of aviation. In the preceding weeks expectation was running high. The press was circling. The eyes of the world were all on the forthcoming occasion.

The French president made dozens of speeches in anticipation of the big day. '*Mes amis*,' he would start, which in Aussie meant 'old mates', '*Mes amis, vous avez . . .*'

About then, Aussies lost the translation but could guess by the way he was waving his arms around that he was bloody excited over what was about to happen.

Finally it was time for the main event. At the airport, as the black tarp was slid from the sleek machine, the crowd went quiet and then collectively gasped.

And so the Concorde was launched. With its backward sloping wings and drooping front end, it was hardly recognisable as an aeroplane. Old people stood about muttering things like, 'Sonic boom, my arse . . . er, derrière, that is', and 'Holy suffering frogs' legs'.

Since Australia was at the forefront of the world's aircraft maintenance, all service work was due to be outsourced to a place not far from the desert town of Birdsville, in a couple of disused stables at the racetrack. The region's suitable atmospheric pressure and lack of humidity made it an obvious choice.

As the time for the first 15 000-kilometre service drew near, Birdsville prepared. However, logistical arrangements had been lacking with reference to the length of the airstrip: the Concorde was unable to land at the far end of the runway and taxi up to the fence at the pub. It was forced to approach from the south, touch down at the pub and, at the other end of the runway, disappear into the shimmering sandhills for about a kilometre. That was a bit of a bummer because the pilot had radioed through to have a pot of Fourex bitter ale waiting for him at the bar, where he was to meet Ray and Stan, the aircraft mechanics. By the time the pilot had taxied back, the beer was hot and flat so the publican generously sold him another at half price.

The fanfare that had met the Concorde's arrival hadn't been anywhere like the sort in France but it was no less enthusiastic. Forty-one people and eight dogs had attended. Four kangaroos and two emus on the strip had necessitated a couple of low-level passes to get them to piss off, and a few dozen corellas had got sucked into the turbines.

In due course all the little glitches were sorted out and things got serious around the bar. It was some time later before the mechanics remembered they had only the afternoon to do the service before take off at dawn the next morning.

'Won't be too bad, Stan. We'll just open the fence here and let ourselves through, we'll idle her out to the track and get on with it.'

'Nah, no rush. Not a hell of a lot to do, mate. I've had a bit of look at the service manual – grease and oil, check the carby, and Pierre's your uncle.'

His mate nodded, drained his beer, grabbed a shifter and a roll of insulation tape and off they went.

As predicted they were nearly finished within the hour. Everyone knows first services are a piece of piss, and all that was left to do was to tighten the bung in the bottom of the carby. But Stan, trying to hurry the process, cross-threaded the bloody thing and about 20 litres of fuel leaked out before he could close it off properly.

'Have a sniff of this, mate. The bloody stuff smells all right, doesn't it?' Stan said, licking a finger at the same time.

'Yeah, like alcohol. What's it taste like?'

'Whisky. Here, what do you make of it?' Stan said as

he loosened the bung back off a bit.

'Give us a proper slug,' Ray replied as he emptied his water bottle and put it under the flow.

About a litre later the pair was flying high, so to speak.

'I'm taking some of that stuff home,' Stan said, wobbling about a bit.

'Me too.'

At around eight o'clock that evening Ray was lying back in his bed feeling no pain when the phone rang. Stan was on the other end.

'That you, Ray? How are you, old buddy? Old mate, thersh's a bit of a problem with that avgas.'

'What would that be, mate? I've had a bit of a go at it. Going down a treat.'

'Is your nose getting longer?'

'Hang on, I'll check. Well . . . er, yes, as a matter of fact, and it seems to be drooping a bit.'

'What about your arms – are they sloping back?

'Funny you should say that. Just popped a couple of buttons off my shirt. What's the go?'

'Dunno, mate, but for Christ's sake, don't fart. I'm ringing you from Hong Kong.'

———

Femmes Fatale

'Eau de Toilette, mate,
That'll freshen Fifi up a bit.'

Sausage sizzle

Darlene was worried. George had been forty and she'd been twenty when they tied the knot. Having such a big difference in age had never caused any problems. Till now anyway.

The bright sparks of their youth had become embers, and they were fizzling out quickly. More particularly the ember of George's member was losing its glow. What he got up, with a bit of trouble that was, wouldn't stay up. But Darlene, at forty, was as randy as she had been at twenty.

I could have an affair, she thought. The fantasy only briefly stimulated her. *Nah, not my go. Sizzling, yes; adulteress, no. I'll have to do what I can.*

'No, it's not for me. It's for my daughter,' Darlene said as she held the flimsy garment up against her.

'What size is she?'

'About my size.'

'Cup size?'

'Yes, about my size.'

The elderly assistant gave a knowing look with the

hint of a smile before saying, 'It's all right, dear. It's not long since I tried to resurrect my love life, but Herb told me not to be so bloody stupid.' Then she added, 'But I'm a lot older than you. And bloody old Herb is over sixty. Over the hill I'm afraid.'

'Oh ... ,' was all Darlene said.

George said he was impressed with the negligee but, even so, bypassed her, brushed his teeth, reached for the Listerine and gargled. As if that wasn't enough, he'd barged in under the bedclothes and was snoring before she'd locked the cat in and the dog out.

What next?, she thought.

No doubt the *New Idea* had some good recipes ... it also featured bikinis filled, no, partly filled with pretty girls. Darlene thought that a strategically opened magazine placed on the arm of George's rocker might spur him on. It did. It prompted him to pick it up and flick to the back and start on the crossword.

I know, she thought, *I'm not done yet.* Extreme situations require stern measures of control.

'Bangers and mash for tea tonight, George.'

'You know the way to a man's heart, don't you, love?' *And somewhere else too*, she thought, as she sprinkled crushed Viagra over his sausages and covered them with gravy.

Darlene took her beloved's meal into the dining room with the words, 'You start without me, Georgie boy. I just want to make sure the custard for the steam pudding doesn't boil over. Won't be more than a few minutes.'

And she waited. But not for long.

'Holy snapping crawdads, Darlene. Look at this. Never seen the likes of it.'

'I'll be there in a sec,' she smiled knowingly, becoming excited herself.

'Best show I've had for a long while. Come and have a look before it's all over.'

Not likely, she nearly said aloud, then answered, 'Hang on.'

'What a bloody turn out, Darlene.'

'What's going on in there?'

'You won't believe it. One banger's on its end, springing up and down on the spot and the other's bounced off my plate onto the floor, and right now it's tearing round the lounge room after the cat.'

———

Glitterati

All her young life, Marilyn had sought fame and fortune. Dreams of glamour, acclaim, the catwalk, TV and film contracts and adoring fans consumed her teens. Well, sorry, Marilyn, no go.

But accountants can rise to dizzy heights too. In due course Marilyn became the boss of a company. She led a hectic life of running board meetings, travelling internationally and attending conferences. It was rewarding for sure but the shining light in her life was her eighteen-year-old daughter, Chantelle, conceived when Marilyn was sixteen. Mother and daughter were frequently mistaken for sisters. Being aware of her mother's busy schedule, Chantelle often took on the role of personal assistant.

'Mum, have you been to the doctor for your smear test yet? Why do you keep putting it off?'

'I will do it, sweetheart. I just haven't had time.'

'Make time, Mum. It's important.'

'I will, promise.'

The following week: the same conversation. And the

next. Finally Chantelle took the lead.

'Mum, your appointment with Dr Susan is at half past two this afternoon. You said this morning on the phone that you would be back from lunch by two, and that you had nothing scheduled until a board meeting at three thirty.'

'Oh, but —'

'No buts. Do it, Mum, or ring up and cancel it yourself. You'll never get around to it if I don't do something.'

'All right then. You win. Would it be okay if I called by your flat and had a freshen-up? I won't have time to go home before the appointment.'

'Course it would, Mum. Just don't leave the bathroom in a mess like you do at your place, and keep out of my wardrobe.'

So, running a touch late, Marilyn raced into the flat and had a quick shower. Then followed deodorant, a generous spray of Femfresh, a quick hair comb, makeup touch-up, fresh lipstick, a whiff of perfume and off down the steps. Fifteen minutes flat. She was used to doing things fast, and well. That's why she was chairwoman of the board.

'Oh, hello, Marilyn,' said the receptionist. 'How are you? I'll be with you in a minute or two.'

She finished the paperwork, swiped Mrs Murphy's Visa card and turned to Marilyn. 'I'm so sorry. Dr Susan has had to go off early; she's nearly dying of the flu. I tried to ring you but your mobile was diverted. I've tentatively booked you in with Dr Martin. Would you be comfortable seeing him?'

'Mmm, I guess so. Dr Martin is very professional, I know. I was with him years before Dr Susan joined the practice. It's just a female thing. You know.'

'Absolutely. I'd do the same myself. Would you like me to reschedule?'

'No, no. It will be quite fine. Truly. If I don't have it done now, it won't happen for another twelve months. And Chantelle won't talk to me for a week.'

'Oh, hello, Marilyn. How are you? Keeping well by the looks,' Dr Martin said cheerily. 'What can I do for you?'

'I was booked for a smear test with Dr Susan. But you'd know she's gone home sick. The receptionist asked me if I'd switch to you.'

Checking Marilyn's file Dr Martin said, 'Yes, you're certainly due.' He stood up and moved towards the door of the treatment room. 'I'll just be a moment. Everything off below the waist, and up on the couch.

You'll find a sheet there you can use to cover yourself.'

A few moments later he returned, and as he lifted the bottom half of the sheet, he said quietly, 'You've gone to a lot of trouble today.'

Momentarily Marilyn was puzzled but then thought, it must be my new French perfume that everyone has been commenting on lately.

However, she felt herself go lobster-red when she went to get dressed and discovered that instead of using Chantelle's Femfresh she'd sprayed herself liberally with her hair glitter.

———

Meals on wheels

'Three score and ten, my arse,' Old Dougie had proclaimed to all and sundry at the local bowls-club dinner. '*Four* score and ten more like it. I reckon I'll still be getting it up then.'

His long-suffering wife, Daph, had shot him a sceptical look. 'You stupid old bugger, you've been having trouble keeping it up for years,' she'd said with a laugh.

'Crucify me in front of our friends, why don't you?'

'Well, you brought the subject up.'

No answer had come as he gave his steak his full attention.

Doug had always had an eye for the female form, and the imagination to go with it. Daph had a good imagination too and she needed every bit of it being married to Doug. But he was a good-hearted, generous soul.

To be fair though, not all that long ago, Daph had been overheard saying, 'Yeah, the old boy is still pretty good on the horizontal exercise, to use his expression.'

'Oh . . .' one listener had said.

'Go on . . .' had said another, obviously filing the information away for future reference.

And the other one had said nothing but a faraway look came into her eyes.

But since then the years had, in fact, started to tell. Obviously it'd been worrying Doug because one day he confided to his bride of fifty years, 'Daph, I don't know how much longer I can keep this up.'

She gave him a look that surely meant, *thank Christ for that*. However, what she actually said was, 'Why is that, lovey?'

'I have arrived at a point in time when I need to have my sex lowered. These days it's all in my head.'

Her concerned look and understanding demeanour,

while comforting, didn't seem to completely allay his fears, so she continued, 'Exactly where it should be at your age, Dougie.'

Then the unspeakable happened. Dear Daph wobbled about, made an ugly face, looked frantic, clutched at her chest, and fell arse over head, dead – just like that, out like a light.

And that gave Dougie something else to think about apart from the state and whereabouts of his dick. Actually there was nought to worry about at all, as it turned out. There was nothing left in his head to lower. And he didn't even miss it.

What he *did* miss when he thought of Daph was good food. No doubt he had loved her – nearly as much as her cooking. So now Meals on Wheels was his top priority. While Dougie appreciated the midday meal, it lacked variety: meat, three veg, custard and jelly. Day in, day out.

Dougie's old mates had been stalwarts since Daph died, and never a day went by that there wasn't some contact. For that he was eternally grateful. They helped with all sorts of little trials, invited him for dinner, took him on bus and fishing trips, anything they could think of. And slowly Dougie came alive. A new man, a late bloomer, or a second bloomer anyway.

One day, after delivering Dougie home from their trip to Cairns, his mates got to thinking that as Dougie had been rejuvenated so might his private areas.

Five years after Daph had died, Dougie's cobbers decided to give him a surprise birthday present: they all put in and agreed to send a stripper to his doorstep.

When the doorbell rang, Dougie toddled to the front door to answer it, fully expecting to see Val from Meals on Wheels with his lunch tray. As he swung open the door, in stepped a gorgeous brunette wearing an equally stunning long fake-fur coat.

Before he'd even got a word out, she held open the fur coat to reveal that she was stark naked underneath – and what a body!

Dougie's jaw dropped and his eyes popped. 'Who are you?'

'I'm here to fulfil your fantasy,' she announced. 'Do you want super sex?'

'I'll have the soup, thanks,' Dougie replied.

———

Laundry maid

If Jack had wanted to be a nurse, he guessed he would have become one, but just lately he was pleased that he hadn't taken it on. He'd had a fair bit to do with hospitals but he'd always been on the receiving end of the enema.

But last month the tables were turned. Beloved wife, Kathleen (the self-diagnosing worst patient type) had to face the knife. Not a terminal condition but a moderately complex procedure. Even so, she had herself psyched up that after the Thursday scalpel exercise, she and Jack would be off to the beach for the weekend: a gallop along the boardwalk, coffee at the other end, and fish and chips for lunch.

Sounded too good to be true. It was. The next three weeks were harrowing for her. They weren't exactly a walk in the park for Jack either. The first week wasn't too bad for him. She didn't want anything much to eat. She slept a lot. Jack didn't run out of clothes. There was still some food in the fridge. Overall, pretty easy really.

It was halfway through the second week when she rose from her sick bed that the rot set in.

'You'll need to do a bit of shopping,' she said.

There's still some plain flour in the cupboard and some celery in the fridge, Jack thought.

'You'll need to do a bit of washing,' she said.

There is a blue singlet and a pair of overalls in my cupboard, Jack remembered.

'Why do you leave the clothes pegs on the line?'

'Why not?'

'Because you just don't, and you don't fold towels like truck tarps either.'

'Oh? Why not? They stack better and one flick and they're unfolded,' Jack answered, thinking she must be getting better.

'No, it *wouldn't* be easier to vacuum the carpet with the leaf blower.'

'Sorry, just a thought.'

But she had a relapse. Obviously keeping him in line regarding housework was more strenuous than she'd thought. So he mixed her up a batch of tablets and put her back to bed again. Consequently he became a dab hand at most things. However he blew it when he was changing the sheets on their bed.

'Kathleen,' he called, 'does the fitted sheet go on the top or the bottom?'

She nearly busted her stitches.

Feminine carpentry

I'll go home and invent a bloody octagonal wheel, Peter thought. *Can't be any worse than this friggin' thing*. He'd heard that one in three supermarket trolleys have square wheels. He thought the odds might be about fifty-fifty in this case as he proceeded down the aisle at the local foodstore one Saturday afternoon.

'Pete, would you be a darling and go along to the next aisle and pick up a few items for me, please? I'll meet you down at fruit and veg,' she asked.

How could he say no? 'Good as done, dearest.' *Augurs well for later in the evening*, he thought. 'What do we need?'

'Here,' she said, producing a notebook. 'I'll write them down. *Talc powder – Johnson's. Soap – Palmolive. Colgate toothpaste – Total Advanced. Tampax Regular.*

Double take. 'What?! Not on your life. What if somebody sees me?'

'So . . .'

'So, what if somebody sees me?' he said.

'You're a big boy now. Meet you down in fruit and veg, you wuss,' she replied, tearing out the leaf.

Bumpety, bumpety, bumpety. Stop. Toothpaste, yep; soap, Lux will do; Johnson's powder, okay.

Now for the tampons. Is this the place?

Hell. There's a girl coming along from the other end of the aisle. Cruise right past women's toiletries, slowly, nonchalantly, but looking hard. Christ, there're thousands of the bloody things.

Bumpety, bumpety to end of aisle.

About turn. Cruise past again, hang over back of trolley looking bored till grandma and two kids go by … eyes like quicksilver. Which bloody ones?

Deep breath. Furtive demeanour. Feel like Uncle Arthur. Here we go. 'Tampax Regular'. Three big packs, no, four . . . save coming back. That wasn't so bad after all.

'Thank you, Peter. Couldn't you find any *Palmolive* soap? Don't worry. You've done well. I'll have to bring you more often. Jeez, I'm not going to run out of these for a while, am I?'

There are lots of things that go on in my life, Peter thought, *but from this moment on shopping for tampons will not be one of them.*

'Bloody hell, how long will it take us to get through here? Look at the line-up,' Peter exclaimed.

'Mr Impatience, relax. Why are you in such a hurry?'

'To get out of here.'

'What, to get home to watch *The Simpsons*?'

'I'm not coming again.'

'Don't you like food? I've got to do this every week.'

As his wife unpacked their trolley, Peter made an idle observation.

'Shit, the checkout chick needs a bomb under her.'

He watched as she picked up the packet of Tampax and turned it over slowly. Unable to find what she was looking for, she reached for the microphone.

Ding! Nasal boredom. 'Checkout four, price on Tampax.' *Ding! Ding!*

Scan, scan, pack, pack.

Look at her watch.

Scan, pack. Observe broken fingernail.

Still no response.

Ding! Drawl slightly louder.

Ding! 'Price on Tampax.' Ding!

Then a young male voice answered loudly from along aisle three. 'What sort are you after? The ones you push in with your thumb or the ones you bang in with a hammer.'

Wide eyed, Peter looked at his wife. The girl on the checkout, shocked out of her boredom, look startled. Two women laughed and two others looked at their feet.

With that, the pimply lout from Stores appeared around the end of the aisle holding up two different packets of thumb tacks – one in each hand.

'These or these?' he inquired.

'You idiot, Kevin. I said "Tampax".'

———

Tarzan and Jane

Surveying his camp on his first overhead circuit for the morning, Tarzan, swinging on a handy vine, yodelled his favourite refrain with less than his usual gusto. Impressing Jane was getting harder to do these days. So, he decided that rather than describing his normal circular pattern, he'd vary the routine. He would perform an oblique elliptical orbit and, as he swung back and forth, to show off his new loin cloth he'd cut in a bit closer to where his beloved was sitting. Jane was sure to admire his ingenuity and his rather becoming attire.

During a few tryouts, he gained momentum and became more and more confident. At the bottom of his arc, when he was just beside his betrothed, his loincloth slipped to one side and she was given a bit of a preview.

Disconcerted by Jane's lack of response and somewhat put off, Tarzan had been less than careful as the full travel of the vine entered the scrub.

Smack! Fair into the trunk of a bloody big ironbark.

'*Ahhh!* Jane, help!'

Tarzan's injuries didn't appear to be life-threatening and Jane wasn't too concerned until she peeped under his loincloth.

'Darling, this is damn serious. Your willy's totally missing.'

'Bugger the old fella,' Tarzan said, blindly patting where his shoulder used to be. 'Look! I've lost an arm. And I can't see properly.'

'Not good news, I must confess. You'd better get going over to the witchdoctor.'

'A slight bingle with a tree trunk. Can you fix me up, Doc?' Tarzan explained.

'Course, mate. Haven't been stumped yet. Right, now, let's see: I'm fresh out of human eyes. No donors lately. Only got the eye of an eagle; is that any good to you?'

'Yep, she'll do.'

'Now, the arm . . . Mmm. No human arms. Thought I had one here somewhere. No, I remember now. That friggin' hyena ate it. I forgot to tie the mongrel up the other night.'

Tarzan had been thinking that while he could have perhaps got by with only one eye, it would be a real bastard having to spend the rest of his life swinging in circles with only one arm. As it was, it had taken him three hours to get to the witchdoctor's surgery instead of the usual one.

'Arm of a chimp is the best I can do, Tarze. Sorry about that. Better than nothing, though.'

'Bloody oath, mate. Sew her on.'

'Now,' the witchdoctor said, 'here's the challenge. *No dicks at all!* Bummer, but I'll see what I can do.'

Doc turned away and disappeared into the adjoining cave. He was away for nearly half an hour.

'Here you go,' he said, when he returned, beaming with pride. 'What do you reckon about this?'

'Holy suffering dung beetles,' Tarzan said excitedly, 'A baby elephant's trunk. Will the missus be stoked with this! Thanks, Doc.'

'Don't mention it, mate. Cost you a warthog. See you in a month. *Next, please.*'

Thirty days later, on the knocker, Tarzan was off again to see the witchdoctor.

'How'd you go?' the MD asked, looking over his patient and inspecting the healed stiches with obvious pride.

'No bloody good. No good at all.'

'What? The eagle eye not up to expectation?'

'Nothing wrong with it. It's a beauty. Spot a tsetse fly on a cheetah's balls at seventy clicks.'

'The chimp arm then?'

'Yeah, real good. A vine snaps and before I can go down with it, the arm's reached up to grab a higher one. Groundbreaking technology, mate. Can't complain about it at all. No, it's that baby elephant's trunk. Can't do a thing with it. Bloody disaster.'

'How can that be so, Tarze? It looks so good.'

'I agree and I'm mighty pleased with the way it looks. But whenever I swing through the jungle and have to swoop a bit low, it reaches down, grabs a trunk full of grass and leaves and jams the lot fair up my arse.'

———

Wedgie

Charlie struggled with the concepts of God and the afterlife.

His wife, Samantha, prevailed on him to become an avid churchgoer like herself. He would argue that since he lived by Christian principles, he had no need.

'You're an atheist heathen,' she'd exclaim, which tended to alter his sunny disposition on occasion.

To appease Sammy, Charlie agreed to attend church once a month. As a trade-off, on the other three Sundays he would be allowed to see how many stubbies of beer he could drink while she was away. It wasn't exactly what Samantha had envisioned, but nevertheless it was a starting point. She would wear him down. In the stakes of unarmed combat her superior weight advantage of some thirty kilos most often won out. Finally, the new arrangements were in place: one week in four of divine worship for Charlie set in stone, no ifs or buts.

With whalebone corset and victory over Charlie firmly in place, Sammy's pious powder-puff expression accompanied the rest of her down the steps to the kitchen on the first Sunday of the month to await her beloved's company to St Patrick's.

'Are you nearly ready, Charles? It's time to go.'

'Go where?'

'To church.'

'When?'

'Now.'

'Not likely, dearest. I'll accompany you in three weeks time. One Sunday per month as agreed. Today I'm ducking down to the boozer. Want a lift to church on the way?'

Finally, on the appointed Sunday, the loving couple walked halfway down the aisle, Sammy leading her heathen, and peeled off to the left. They sat on a pew behind Mrs Holloway, who turned three-quarters around, smiled at Samantha and glared at Charlie.

'Good morning to you too,' he responded.

'Huh!' she added to her previous welcome.

Charlie settled himself and immediately boredom overtook him. However, soon after, as the congregation stood for the first hymn, his train of thought, or lack of it, was interrupted. If Mrs Holloway had known what lay behind her, or more importantly, what she presented in front of Charlie, she mightn't have been singing 'Onward Christian Soldiers' with such enthusiasm.

A considerable proportion of her gathered polyester skirt had become tightly wedged in the crack of her huge rear end. Charlie glanced sideways at his wife, but given that she kept her eyes trained on the heavens, Sammy gave the impression of being unaware of the situation.

Charlie pondered the state of affairs for a while – in fact he could think of little else – before he made a decision. He didn't like Mrs Holloway. It was very obvious that the sentiment was reciprocated, but it seemed only reasonable to a decent Christian man that he should help her out.

Accordingly, he reached forward and tugged firmly at the wedgie to release it. Sammy reacted before Mrs Holloway did. She turned towards Charlie, bearing an arcing left haymaker that caught him flush on the left side of his kisser. A bloody beauty.

That left Charlie's head in an unenviable open-spaced position that was quickly filled by Mrs Holloway's left-cross open hander as she turned 180 degrees. It caught him flush on the other side of his mug. It was a wonder at that moment that the rapid-fire treatment hadn't squeezed his head to a point.

A month later.

'For Christ's sake, Charlie, what happened?' his supervisor asked on Monday morning. 'Last month at church you got a swollen, bruised cheek after pulling some old duck's dress out of her bum crack. And this time a black eye. You'll have to keep away from church.'

'Well,' Charlie explained, 'after last time, I figured she must have wanted her dress in her bum crack, so yesterday I pushed it back in for her.'

———

Top Blokes

'Scrubber throwing
not your forté,
I take it?'

Tim and I

It was advertised far and near. It was in every newspaper, city and provincial – *The Courier Mail* in Brisbane, the *Sydney Morning Herald*, *The Age*, the *NT News*, the *Westralian*, *The Advertiser* and the one in Tassie – on every radio station – the ABC, 2UE, 4KQ – and every TV channel; the whole bloody shooting match. But the news travelled best by word of mouth. The country was alive with speculation.

'Hear ye! Hear ye! Don't miss the greatest poetry competition in the history of Australia. There'll be prizes the worth of which has been unheard of in this country. No, this not a gimmick. Phone the Prime Minister's Department for verification. The main prize will be awarded for the best stanza, rhyming couplet or limerick.'

Entries totalled over 30000. Judging took place over a period of three months with assessors working twelve-hour shifts seven days a week.

Then the end was near. The long list gave hope to some and disappointment to others. The short list made a few hearts bounce. Finally, it came down to two contestants – a man of the cloth and a man of the saddle, a retired drover – but there was a glitch. It was a hung jury.

In accordance with the Trade Practices Act and stipulations from the Office of Fair Trading, there was to be a showdown on live TV, broadcast nationally. The audience's reaction would decide the winner. The logistics included locking each contestant in a soundproof room while the other performed. As each contestant was led out onto the studio floor, he would be given a single word, with which his stanza had to end.

Being used to giving sermons, the preacher volunteered to go first. He bowled out looking confident and beamed at the audience.

'The word is "Timbuktu". You have thirty seconds,' the judge advised.

The priest steepled his hands as if praying, looked to the heavens, and then straight off the top of his head recited:

'Been a preacher for many a long year,
preached in parishes far and near:
from Dublin town to Paraburdoo
from Brisbane city to Timbuktu.'

The audience roared, amazed at the man's quick

response. There was little doubt as to the winner without them even needing to hear the other contestant.

The preacher stood aside and waited for his adversary to make a fool of himself.

The door to the soundproof room was opened, and the judge said, 'Next, please.' Old Bill, the drover, appeared slowly in the doorway, pulled his hat down over his eyes to adjust to the lights, looked this way and that, and checked for solid footing before ambling across the stage towards the vacant chair.

'Be seated, sir,' the judge offered.

'No, mate, she'll be right. Won't be here long. What have I got to do?'

'When I give you a word, you'll be required to compose a stanza ending with that word. You'll have thirty seconds to do so.'

The old cattleman nodded, then said to no one in particular as he squinted at the battery of lights, 'Need a bloody good floodlight like that for night-loading cattle onto the semitrailer.'

'Right, on with the job,' the judge said. 'The word is "Timbuktu".' Click went his stopwatch. The drover, who'd been leaning against the wall, now dropped to his haunches. He fished out his tobacco, expertly rolled a smoke and lit it. He closed his eyes as he drew on the fag. Twenty-two seconds gone.

'Stage fright,' they whispered. 'Just plain dumb,' one suggested.

With only two seconds to go before they cracked him off, Bill opened his eyes and drawled:

'Tim and I a-drovin' went;
espied three sheilas in a tent.
They said nicely, "How do you do?"
So I bucked one and Timbuktu.'

There was a stunned silence before the crowd erupted. Then it rose to a standing ovation that vibrated the cobwebs from the ceiling. Old Bill was declared the winner as the preacher went red, two blue-haired matrons left the studio in disgust, and the judge nearly busted the stitches over his hernia. The drover said, 'Better go. Tim's waiting for me out the back with the horses.'

———

Passport to nowhere

Two Yanks were planning to visit Australia for a safari holiday and they'd hired a tour guide for their month-long adventure. They were let down from the outset when they didn't see mobs of kangaroos streaking away from Sydney airport as their jumbo landed. They were even more disappointed on presenting themselves at Avis Car Rentals to find no guide waiting as arranged.

'Dang it, girl,' the bigger bloke said. 'There's supposed to be a guide here to meet us with a four-wheel drive ranch wagon. His name is apparently Bluey somebody. What sort of a fool name is that anyway?'

'I'm sure Bluey's here somewhere, sir,' the counter girl replied. 'You can't miss him; he's got a big red beard. He took delivery of your vehicle an hour ago.'

'Waal, he's not here now, is he? What will we do?'

Patiently she explained that the car was in Bay 38, and the guide would probably be with it. With that, the Americans took her advice and, each trailing about six cubic metres of luggage on trolleys, finally located Bluey, asleep in the driver's seat with his head slumped forward onto a newspaper covering the steering wheel.

The smaller Yank shook him by the shoulder and woke him.

'Ah, g'day fellas,' Blue said. 'Reckoned you'd have to be along soon. Throw your bags in the back. I'll unlock it for you . . . and I'll fold up me newspaper and put me boots on while you pack your stuff in.'

As it turned out, while Blue wasn't into mollycoddling clientele nor pissing in their pockets, he was a brilliant bushman and wonderful guide. In his company the outback came alive. Never in their wildest dreams could the Yanks have imagined the sights and sounds of the bush to which they were introduced: the secret Aboriginal paintings, rare marsupials, strange birds, awesome night skies, camp cooking par excellence – the whole shebang. So impressed were they that on the second or third last day of their holiday they pooled their remaining resources to give Blue a tip so huge it nearly caused him to utter, 'Oh, you really shouldn't have.' Instead he corrected himself and said, 'Thanks; want another stubby?'

Backtracking now towards Sydney, still out Bourke way but making good time, the visitors fell quiet. The anticlimax was upon them. Time to go home.

'Shit!' Blue exclaimed. As their Toyota wagon had rounded a bend, a red kangaroo as tall as a medium-sized giraffe materialised from nowhere. There he was, standing stock-still, in the middle of the bitumen, minding his own business, when Blue anchored out and slammed into him.

Unhurt but a bit shaken up, the three occupants climbed out.

'Dead,' Blue pronounced as he felt for the roo's pulse with his boot. 'Dead as a maggot, poor bugger. Just having a bit of a look around his backyard, and the next thing arse over head. Never know when your number's up.'

With that Blue grabbed the roo and started to drag it over to the side of the road, towards the drain.

'Hang on, man,' said the Yank with the smaller hat. 'Here, sit that – what do you call them again, Bluey? Yeah, that's right – sit that boomer up against the back wheel and I'll put my arm around its neck. It'll make one hell of a trophy to show them back home, won't it, Hank.'

Hank agreed and it seemed reasonable to Blue. The customer's always right.

So Hank set up his half-million-dollar tripod and finally all was in readiness.

'No, hold it,' said his companion. 'Wait. I'll put my coat on it.' This he did and buttoned it up to the collar. He tried his hat for size too but it seemed a little loose so that idea was discarded.

He then positioned himself beside the kangaroo's corpse, placing an arm casually around its neck.

'Okay, man. Shoot.'

At which point the kangaroo regained its senses,

leapt up, and without a backwards glance took off and cleared the roadside fence. It shot across the gully, cleared another fence and was observed entering a four- or five-thousand-acre wheat paddock at the speed of light.

'Goddamn, Bluey! Run down that kangaroo.'

'He's all yours, mate,' Blue said, with his boot on the second bottom wire of the fence pushing down, and a hand under the third wire pulling up, 'You have a go if you like. I'll put the billy on. You might be away for a bit.'

'Damn it. Do something. My passport and my wallet are in that coat.'

Blue pondered a second. 'Can't help with the passport, old buddy, but I might be good for a small loan.'

———

Sweet revenge

Barney and Sam and their two sons had had a gutful. Every Monday morning they surveyed the damage that had been done. Their pineapple farm was suffering. It was obvious that louts on motorbikes had roared up and down the carefully prepared planting beds, along and across the drills when no one was around. No regard for freshly planted suckers and tops was taken. It would have to stop.

Smoko time this particular morning saw the men all sitting about, tearing into tradesmen's tucker like they'd not been fed for a fortnight.

Vrrrrrooom! Vrrrrooomm! The sound from over the hill indicated that the bike riders were at it again, ruining a neighbouring patch. They were becoming cheekier – appearing during the working week now as well.

It wasn't Barney and Sam who got up from their seats in the shed, it was their two sons. One of them was built like a two-storey brick shithouse and the big bloke dwarfed him. They would give chase and perhaps an attitude adjustment to the perpetrators.

By the time they'd boarded the LandCruiser, the noise had died down and they assumed the vandals had departed the scene of the crime. Not so. At speed they came upon the two louts, who had dismounted, taken off their helmets and were sitting casually on the edge of a raised bed, obviously deciding what to damage next.

Such was their surprise that they leapt up, mounted their bikes and gunned away, minus helmets.

'Hmm,' said the big son as he turned one discarded helmet over in his hand.

'I've got an idea,' said the extra-big son. 'Listen to this . . .'

It might be assumed that people who start their days early, with perhaps a cup of tea and a slice of toast, and follow that with a substantial smoko at about 9.30 a.m. could reasonably expect to have to heed the call of nature by about 9.50 a.m., and the battery of farts let loose indicated that the sons were right on schedule. Time to put the plan into action.

In a totally cleared forty-acre paddock, they stepped either side of the ute – for privacy – each carrying a helmet. There was always a toilet roll behind the ute seat for emergencies. For added effect they pulled out the helmets' inner linings, relieved themselves, and then replaced the linings.

Returning the helmets to where they'd found them, they retreated to the top of the rise to observe what took place next.

Right on cue, two bikes roared along the farm road. The riders espied their helmets, where they'd left them, slammed them on their heads and tore off in jubilation . . . never to be seen again.

———

Not guilty, yer Honour

'Poddy dodging' is another name for 'moonlighting', which can also be termed 'lifting cattle'. Then there's 'gully raking', 'duffing' and 'rustling', but they all mean the same – stealing cattle.

Harry Redford was Australia's most notorious cattle thief. He entered folklore when he lifted 1000 head of cattle from Bowen Downs at Longreach in 1870. His feat of droving the cattle through three states on unmade stock routes caught the imagination of every rural dweller in the country. He might have got away with it too but for one white bull, which was reputed to have followed the herd and rejoined it much later. Harry was charged with stealing only that bull. But he wasn't convicted. After that dubious verdict, the town erupted in outrage; it became like the wild west, and the District Court was suspended for two years as a consequence. These are facts.

What happened to Pat and Mick might be factual too. On the other hand, well . . .

'Patrick, me lad, we're never going to get on in this world without a kick along. I can't bear the thought of digging ditches for the rest of me life.'

'What might you be having in your mind to do about it, me mate?'

'Ah, to be sure, we could try to rob the bank again. It not be our fault we got locked in the strong room for two days while we counted the money.'

Mick wasn't totally enamoured of a re-run and put his mind to some alternative.

'We could steal the six Hereford steers from the police station yard – the ones they're going to use for evidence in that duffing case. They've already been stolen. Knocking them off again shouldn't matter all that much. Perhaps we could hide under the lock-up till the sergeant falls asleep tonight.'

'P'haps. But where would we get rid of them?' Pat queried.

'First things first.'

Pat was sceptical and Mick had to convince him.

'We'll get them out onto the road and then we might have to wait under the street light till dawn. While we're there, we'll have plenty of time to discuss how to dispose of them. Where's your ticker, me old mate?'

And so it came to pass. And it also came to pass that the guileless lawbreakers were apprehended that same evening.

On the following Monday morning Pat and Mick,

looking decidedly dejected, were before Magistrate Murphy.

The Crown evidence was extensive. It consisted of, 'Patrick O'Donnell and Michael O'Dwyer did you steal the cattle?'

'No, yer Honour.'

'I believe you did. Where are they?'

'Yer Honour, there is no evidence against us. The cattle all ran off into the bush.'

'I shall consider your statement. We shall adjourn for a quarter of an hour,' the beak Murphy said, 'and then I shall deliver my verdict.'

Pat and Mick fair shat themselves till the verdict was given.

'Not guilty,' said the magistrate, 'so long as you bring the cattle back. And O'Donnell, how might your mother be back in Tipperary?'

———

Flying high

'You're what?' You're buying *what*?'

'Be reasonable, Betty. It's not as if they've got a motor. Hardly anybody ever gets hurt. Hang-gliders are pretty safe.'

'How much are they?'

'About half the price of a Brahman bullock.'

'How much is that exactly?'

'Well, the market's down a fair bit but normally it would be about the same price as six equipped water-troughs and 2000 metres of inch-and-a-quarter low-pressure polypipe.'

'Get the bloody thing if you want it. You won't be happy until you do. I'm going into the office to check your insurance.'

The great day came when it was delivered via the mail truck. Kevin was taken aback by the dead weight of the unassembled contraption. In the magazines they looked as light as feathers floating about. *Ah well*, he thought, *what's done is done*.

Kev had an idea for his maiden voyage: taking off from Uluru. There was precious little other high ground for hundreds of kilometres and it should be easy enough to pick up a thermal from that height, he reckoned. But as he prepared for the event, it crossed Kev's mind that by the time he'd lugged the thing all the way up the rock he might be a bit buggered. Kev thought it would make sense to take that smartarse first-year jackeroo with him as a packhorse so he'd be fresh for takeoff.

As they worked their way up the slope, Kev gauged

the altitude and a thread of doubt entered his mind. *Fair way down*, he thought as he peered over the edge. About halfway, the thread had morphed into a cord. Three quarters the way up, and he was starting to shit himself. Vertigo, here we come. By the top he was fair packing it.

'Dunno, young man,' Kev said to the jackeroo. 'You're a fair bit lighter than I am. It might make sense if you have a go first – a test-drive, you know.'

'Bloody oath. I was thinking that myself but I wasn't game to suggest it, you being such a bastard of a boss and all. I'm fitter anyway, and it's a young man's sport.'

The assembly took longer than predicted and the midday thermals had long since dissipated. The boss was bloody pleased he'd given the aircraft over to the jackeroo, the cheeky young bastard.

Finally, lift off! The kid took to it like a professional. Round and round the rock he circled, rising and dipping with the air currents. The boss was green with envy.

But suddenly it all changed. From out of nowhere a great northern wind started to blow. Kev watched as the dust rose and swirled, and the jackeroo and his aircraft were carried up and away into the wide blue yonder. In no time flat the hang-glider and its pilot were nowhere to be seen.

Several hours later, at Maree, maybe a 400 kilometres south of the South Australian border, on the open verandah of a homestead, two old retired stockmen were getting steadily pissed on overproof rum. One exaggerated the size of his droving herd: 6000 cows in one mob plus only 5998 calves because two had been sighted being stuffed into the pouch of a roo as tall as a flagpole. The other claimed he'd witnessed a plague of giant mice, which were so huge they terrified the station cats into climbing the windmill from where they had to be airlifted out with the musterer's chopper.

Then there was an interruption.

'By God, Lew, did you see that?'

'See what?'

'That bloody great shadow that passed over us.'

'You're pissed, Roly.'

'But I'm not blind. Wait till I get the shot gun.'

Just as he emerged the shadow passed over them again.

'Jesus Christ, mate. Look at the size of that wedge-tailed eagle! Wing span the size of a twin-engine Cessna. I'll get the bastard.'

Kaboom! Kaboom! Both barrels.

'Get him?' Lew asked and squinted.

'Nah, but I think I might have winged him a bit.

Any rate, he dropped that bloody great rabbit he was carrying.'

———

Discount king

Everybody liked Toby, even if he only paid his bills three or four times a year. 'I'll get it to you when I can,' he'd say, 'you know how tight money is these days. It's the bloody GST. Place hasn't been the same since.'

To his credit he didn't waste money. He wasn't a drinker or a smoker. He had a ute but preferred to use his bike. He went to bed with the chooks and got up with them to save electricity. That was Toby.

'Square up that account, Toby,' Ron, the new owner at the garage advised. 'We're not a bank.'

'Soon I will,' Toby would promise solemnly, 'as soon as my money comes through.'

The other merchants in town were well used to Toby and most either charged him top dollar for his purchases or added a bit of interest to his accounts, which worried Toby not one bit. All bar Ron, who continually harassed him.

'You'll be gone one day and I'll still be here,' Toby told him. 'Actually, by the way you carry on you'll be gone sooner rather than later.'

'Whether I'm gone or not, the money is owing and I'm going to get the debt collectors onto you.'

'As you will,' Toby said as he cycled off.

Ron was left seething and shaking his fist, and from then on became even more unreasonable. One day, Toby leant his bike against the front wall of the servo and went inside to buy a new puncture-repair kit. While he was thus occupied, Ron scarfed around the side of the servo, grabbed the bike and chained it to the Mobil sign.

'Mmm,' Toby said as he made to walk home.

'You can get your bike back when you pay your account,' gloated Ron.

Toby made no answer.

The following month Toby arrived at the servo, riding a brand-new Malvern Star. Ron eyed Toby quietly as the bike was leant against the wall.

'Things must be looking up, Toby,' Ron said, all friendly. 'Come to pay your bill, I suppose. It'll be good to tidy it up.'

'Yes, Ron, my friend. Thank you for your patience.'

'You can pick up your old bike any time.'

Toby made no reply. He went inside to the girl at the counter and paid the account. On returning, as he went to pedal off, Ron called after him, 'Don't forget to pick up your old bike.'

'Your bike, Ron. You wanted it so much I thought you should keep it. I deducted the cost of this new one from the account.'

———

Fore!

After retirement, golf became Jeff's life. Nothing wrong with that – but how bloody boring, his old mates reckoned. In particular his mate Barney, next-door neighbour and drinking partner of thirty years, was being neglected.

'Come on, Barney, why don't you learn to play?'

'What? Hit a ping-pong ball all over the paddock? Two or three times would be plenty to have a bit of a look at the country. Why the hell you would want to keep on going back, I've got no idea. Waste of time in my book.'

'Yeah, Barney,' Jeff said sarcastically, 'you do set a cracking pace yourself, don't you? Mow the lawn once a fortnight, all day in front of the telly, four-thirty to eight o'clock in the pub.'

'Huh! Get rooted.'

'Come down on Saturday and we'll go eighteen holes. I'm not very good so there's a decent chance you will be better than me. Give it a go, mate.' Finally, after much cajoling Barney agreed.

Two birdies, two pars and 120 other shots to finish the course. Still, pretty good for a beginner, and who was counting anyway?

'You're a natural, Barney,' his mate said after the fifth pot. 'Makings of a champion,' after the eighth. 'Give Tiger a go for his money . . . all the women do anyway – ha ha ha!'

Barney was hooked. In no time he became a reasonable golfer, and it wasn't all that long before he was attempting to coerce his wife, Doreen, into giving the game a go. Then she could accompany him on the days when he couldn't find another partner. She had been even more stubborn that he was, but finally she agreed.

'Come on, Dor, it's not a bloody fashion parade. Let's get going.'

Teeing off from the first, Doreen whacked a controlled slice two-thirds up the fairway, dead centre.

Shit, Barney thought.

Dor's attempt on the second was a bit miserable, but the next four came in pars and birdies, and in contrast Barney was playing like a broken mouth organ.

Doreen continued with her beginner's luck and even potted an ace on the thirteenth.

'Bloody hell, Dor, have you been holding out on me? This isn't funny. Make a fool of a man.'

Barney was starting to get the shits by this time, and he was secretly pleased when Doreen speared one shot off into the rough. They watched as it ricocheted off the branch of a blue gum, scared a couple of scrub turkeys into flight and bounced high, over into a cow paddock where a couple of dairy cows were grazing quietly.

Then the search was on. The ball was a red spot No. 7. They searched high and low, under thickets, in the reeds by the creek, hither and thither, yonder and beyond, and after half an hour were on the brink of admitting failure.

Then from nearby Barney observed a cow raise her tail to have a pee.

'No, couldn't be,' he said aloud as he focused on the rear end of the cow and what looked like a golf ball stuck up its bum.

As he gave it the quick once over, he called to his wife, 'Come over here, Dor. I think I've found it. This one looks like yours.'

———

Turn it up, Dick

'Mum, what do you think about buying that new tractor? Wouldn't mind getting one before I die. Never owned a new tractor. We've only ever had the grey Ferguson we bought in 1958.'

His wife didn't answer for a while.

Dick waited for the inevitable.

'Where's the money coming from? Do you know something I don't?'

His defence was always the same. 'We can borrow it and pay it off with a crop of pumpkins.'

'Well, put in a crop of pumpkins and we'll buy a tractor when we harvest them.' Then she added, 'Why haven't we ever earned enough from a crop of pumpkins to pay for the groceries before?'

'Beats me,' he said. 'You do the books.'

Next day.

'See you've bought one of those new tractors they've been advertising, Bert,' Dick commented over the phone. 'The dealer rang the other day to say there are only three left. Said I'd better hurry if I want one. I told him

I'd have a talk to you. Are they any good?'

'Bloody oath.'

'Plenty of power?'

'Bloody oath.'

'Three-point linkage?'

'What's that?'

'Power-steering?'

'What's that?'

'Red?'

'Bloody oath, mate. Only way to go. Why do you think I bought it?'

With a recommendation like that I can hardly go wrong, Dick thought. He decided against telling Mum he'd placed the order. She'd been feeding the chooks at the time. No sense distracting her from her work.

Dick knew in his own heart that he'd done the right thing. The increased production would soon pay for the tractor. And the finance terms offered by the dealer seemed very reasonable at 20 per cent interest.

'You what!?'

'I thought I'd better tell you, Mum, so as you can make some adjustments to the books.'

'What adjustments? There's nothing to adjust. Ring

up and cancel the order right this minute.'

'Little bit late for that, dear. That's it on the dealer's truck coming through the gate right now.'

But Mum was a tolerant soul, and when she saw the look on Dick's face her heart melted. In fact, as the tractor was being unloaded she felt compelled to put her arm around his waist and say, 'Bugger putting a few dollars away for our old age, Dick. We've been here for years and haven't needed much money yet.'

If he was apprehensive before, fearing some back-lash, he wasn't now. His excitement soared. Then followed the customary detailed operation instructions from the dealer of which Dick heard not a single word. Right, off for a test-drive in the cultivation paddock. Seat adjusted. Clutch engaged. Brake off. And away.

Now Dick, a careful sort who was very tidy around the farm, liked to keep one step ahead by identifying potentially dangerous situations. A few months before, he had unlinked the peg harrows – implements with rows of spikes used to prepare seedbeds – from the old tractor. He'd flipped them over a couple of times and rested them on their edges at a slight angle, lean-ing against the barbed-wire fence, out of harm's way. Hence the top row of pegs, each about 150-millimetres long, protruded through the top and second fence wires.

Unbeknown to Dick, his old pensioner pony had been searching for something at the right height on which to scratch her arse. Brown Bess thought all her Christmases had come at once when she discovered a whole row of bum-scratchers. So energetic had Bess's incessant rubbings become that they'd set the harrows off balance, so they now lay in the long grass, pegs now hidden and facing upwards.

In Dick's eagerness to see the new tractor, he'd pushed the gate to the cultivation paddock open, but not fully. No cause for consternation. There was still plenty of room to pass through, even though it necessitated driving the tractor a little to one side, which would put it in the long grass near the fence for about ten metres.

Not everyone knows that a lot of tractors have their tyres filled with water. There are two reasons: gives them more traction and more weight, which lowers the centre of gravity.

Straight over the pegs Dick drove . . . and punctured all four tyres, sending water spouts from the back tyres heavenward, and the two others from the smaller front tyres forward at a 45-degree angle. Altogether a thoroughly impressive sight.

———

Texas crude

Tex came from Texas. With a name like that, he'd hardly come from Hawaii. Indeed he was in the Australian outback, halfway between the black stump and Snake Gully and not all that far north of the place where the dog shat in the tuckerbox.

'Dang it, man,' Tex said, pushing back a stetson that had a dozen merinos and a kelpie vying for the shadow. 'Back home we've got sheep twice as big as yours and fleece, I tell ya, the fleece is our second-biggest export earner behind oil.'

'That so?' Dad answered, and Dave looked impressed.

'Yes, buddy. And for that matter, three-quarters of the world's oil production comes out of Texas.'

'Yeah?' Dad said quietly. 'Must be a pretty rich place.' Dave's eyes opened wider.

'Sure is. And our cowboys wear the biggest boots and belt buckles in the world. And I see our rodeo bulls make yours look like poddy calves.'

'Must have extra good soil to make them grow so big, eh?'

'Yes, it is. Just let me tell you about our ranches.'

'I can't wait to hear. They'd be big too, I s'pose.'

'They're the biggest in the world.' As he spoke, Tex puffed out his chest and stretched his arms wide. 'It takes a whole day for a horse to walk across them.'

'That's right, is it?' Dad said, as he took out his tobacco and rolled a smoke. As he lit it he said quietly to the blowhard, 'Yeah, we had a lazy bastard of a horse like that once, so we shot it.'

True sportsmen

China had long held a fascination for Sean and his enthusiasm had, over the years, rubbed off on Pat. The fact that the Olympics were about to begin in Beijing excited him, and he persuaded Pat to quickly grab a plane ticket and they'd take off for a bit of a look about. On the very morning Sean sat in front of the computer to book their two tickets the phone rang. By extreme coincidence it was 2UE radio calling to tell Sean that if he could name the marsupial on the Australian coat of arms, he would be the winner of three airfares to Beijing.

After a few moments Sean answered excitedly, 'Emu.'

'No,' said the presenter. 'Close enough, though. We'll send three tickets to you in the mail.'

Now they had a spare ticket. Within hours they found Murphy, full to the gills with Guinness, and took off to Sydney airport.

'We're off to see the Olympics,' they told him when he woke up.

'Where's the toilet?' he answered.

It hadn't crossed the minds of the mates that they might need tickets to get into the venues.

'To be sure, Sean, I'd not been giving it much thought. I thought we might be able to pay at the gate,' Pat said.

Murphy thought he'd heard of a word like 'scalper', and after extensive enquiry, and a few false leads to do with having the top of your head cut off, they finally located a bloke who would sell them tickets for about five times normal price.

During a tense bargaining session, Pat told the scalper to get rooted and Sean questioned the scalper's ancestry as Murphy looked on thoughtfully. The scalper called them a bunch of dickheads and sold the tickets to somebody else. All in all they hadn't progressed far towards gaining entry into the stadium.

However, Sean had an active mind and was not of a persuasion to dally. Quickly, in the cleaner's room beside the men's toilets, he found a broom, broke the head off it and proceeded to the main competitor's gate.

'Javelin,' he said to the gatekeeper, and was allowed to pass.

'Better hurry,' said the bloke, 'I see them limbering up.'

Too easy, Sean thought.

Pat had witnessed his mate's cunning and racked his brain to match it. 'Ah ha!' he said to Murphy. 'Watch this.'

Nearby stood a 1968 Holden Kingswood. Pat used his tobacco tin to flick off the hub cup, which he tucked under his arm. As he passed through the turnstile, he said to the toll keeper, 'Discus, me boy,' and was allowed to pass through with a smile.

Murphy was momentarily stumped. Who could he impersonate? Then it came to him. It took him twenty minutes to roll up a 400-metre strand of barbed wire from the security compound and present himself at the entrance. As he made to pass through, the gatekeeper halted him in his tracks.

'Where do you think you're going with that?' he asked, pointing to the roll of barbed wire slung over Murphy's shoulder.

'Fencing, mate,' Murphy replied. 'My event is about to start.'

———

Bring a Plate

*'The Colonel wasn't wrong – that hot and spicy
leghorn packs a fair punch.'*

Baker's delight

Stock & Station Agents invariably travel fast on deplorable roads to inspect large mobs of cattle on remote properties. They mostly drive top-of-the-range Land-Cruisers for speed and safety.

Their poorer relatives, the company reps selling cattle dip and sheep drench to produce outlets for resale, all drive three-year-old Commodores but, granted, they don't often get off the bitumen, if some of the tarmac they travel on could be termed 'bitumen'.

Stan was one of the company reps. He loved life, his family, his job, and the people he dealt with. He was the purveyor of perpetual good cheer. Stan also loved pasties as a main course, donuts as dessert and cappuccino to wash it all down. His waistline was proof.

Stan's regular Friday run kept him in contact with produce agents across the countryside, and his favourite bakery, by design or luck, was situated 60 kilometres from a couple of the establishments he serviced. Routinely, he'd arrive at the bakery at 10 a.m. on the dot each Friday, to hit up Jack, the pastry cook, for his usual, after having salivated from five kilometres out. It was an arrangement that couldn't have been better until the day Stan was covering a sick colleague's run as well as his own. His usual schedule was thrown; he was running two hours early. No worries: his smoko menu would become breakfast. Same hunger pangs, just on daylight saving's time.

'G'day,' Stan called to the back and shoulders busy at the bench, as he swung open the flyscreen door of the bakery. 'Too early for a couple of pasties and three donuts?'

Didn't think Jack was as tall as that, he thought.

'No, you're right. How yer going?' answered an unfamiliar voice.

'Yeah, good. Is that you, Jack?'

'No, Jack's crook. Be with you in a minute just as soon as I get this batch finished.'

As he waited, Stan gazed about absently before focusing on what was happening behind the counter. The baker appeared to be using two hands to crimp the edges of the pasties. Bit odd.

'Mate, what are you doing there? Never seen them made like that before.'

With that, the locum turned to Stan and looked him full in the face, giving him a gummy grin. In his hands he held two sets of dentures, which he wiped on his flour-covered apron before returning them to his mouth.

'You dirty bugger,' Stan said, appalled, 'haven't you got a tool?'

'Yeah, course I have, but I use it for making the holes in the donuts.'

———

Always eat your greens

Some things never change. And we hope the Carlton Brewery Clydesdale horse team that pulls the wagon loaded with beer barrels will be one of them. Melbourne wouldn't be the same without it.

In days gone by, the Queensland Hoteliers Association had also maintained its own unique tradition.

Every year the publicans in each area, maybe four or five at a time, would gather for a lunchtime meeting. The venue for the meetings rotated around the hotels. Some might say the assemblies were to discuss business, but if any concrete proposals and outcomes had been nutted out or reported, they would have disappeared in the alcoholic haze that settled over the gathering.

This particular day began in the usual style.

'For Christ's sake, Max, steady up. You'll be pissed by lunchtime and it's barely past smoko,' Greg, one of the visiting publicans said to his brother, younger by ten years. 'I shouldn't have asked you to come with me.'

'I can't believe there's so much free booze,' Max answered.

'Go and get yourself a packet of chips or nuts or something. I don't want you getting sick and spewing everywhere.'

'Look after yourself, and I'll do the same.' With that, Max went off and poured another beer from the jug, and Greg went to find someone else to talk to.

Greg could see the writing on the wall but he could do nought to stop it. Max was an adult now and could make his own decisions.

As expected, his brotherly advice went unheeded, substantially unheeded, and Greg was somewhat relieved when he saw Max head off to the toilet. At least that might occupy him for a while. Additionally, if Max was sick, that was the place to be.

As Max emerged from the toilet, Greg took the opportunity to cut him off at the pass and offer a little extra advice. The move seemed less than successful since the sound '. . . k off' then floated across the room and caught the attention of a few.

Fortunately, just then people started to take their seats. Lunch was being served. By contrivance, Greg half camp-drafted his sibling to the end of the long table and sat beside Max, effectively leaving him with no neighbour to whom he could jibber shit. Nor could he reach the beer jug. So far, so good.

T-bone steaks, obviously from a dinosaur, overhung their plates. Mountains of chips, liberal servings of tomato, beetroot and pineapple completed the meal, not forgetting plenty more beer. Quality pub fare as usual.

Either 'gutso' or 'gusto', or both, described the diners' manners.

In due course muffled burps and favourable comment took precedence over talk of the price of beer and cost of delivery.

As the cook did her rounds collecting crockery, cutlery and scraps, she made her way to the end of the table, where Max sat. Although still bleary eyed, he seemed to have sobered up a bit and looked like an afternoon nap wouldn't go astray.

'Enjoy your meal, sir?' she asked genially, 'No complaints?'

'No complaints with the steak but I do have one about the salad.'

She stopped, obviously taken aback.

'Oh?'

'Yes. The lettuce was so limp I couldn't eat it all.' Max pointed to his plate.

'Sir, you weren't served any lettuce. What you have left there is the other half of your green serviette.'

————

Square hooks

Diamantina Lakes in western Queensland is pretty remote country. It's one of Australia's biggest and newest national parks.

Old Jack had taken up part-time residence there. Not where the tourists visit but way to buggery back in the scrub, miles away. He'd knocked up a bit of a humpy and he'd visit regularly, just him and his over-grown pup, Jackson. As far as everybody knew, they'd mooch around the scrub, looking at birds and stars and emus and things.

They said Jackson was the closest thing to a living relative Jack had and thought that perhaps that's how the dog got its name – son of Jack. But maybe that was all bullshit because Jack's proper name was Giuseppe.

Jackson was huge – as big as a Shetland pony or a bit bigger and just as strong, and friggin' smart, and he could swim like a fish as well.

Jack was a fisherman of note. He was the scourge of the barramundi and yellowbelly species, but Jack could only eat so much fish and Jackson didn't like fish at all. He preferred Meaty Bites with extra cereal and added antibiotics.

So what to do with the extra fish? Be a bastard to waste it. Then Jack had a brainwave. Bloody hell, why hadn't he thought of it before? Yes, he might be able to sell some of it. Who could ever know? That his outfit was equipped with an esky the size of an iceberg and a thumping big generator was fortuitous.

There was nothing Jackson liked better than fetching sticks from the water, and one day Jack had another of his light-bulb moments. If Jackson would retrieve sticks, Jack figured the dog probably wouldn't mind fetching a stick trailing a bit of rope . . . and with some training, eventually a bloody big rope with a weight on the end. And finally, if all went to plan, a rope with a net tied onto it. The plan was coming to fruition.

The remaining problem was to educate Jackson not to immediately return to shore – not until Jack had run around the other side of the billabong anyway. He would swim to his master instead. Before Jackson made landfall, Jack would scarper along the bank under the coolibah trees and set Jackson a new target. In due course, man and dog would arrive back at their starting point – with Jackson towing a hundred metres of fishing net jam-packed with all sorts of fish, the odd turtle, eels by the dozen and now and again a little freshwater crocodile – but they were murder on the net.

Over a period Jack built up a thriving business without even getting his feet wet. Early one morning, both man and dog were busy at their respective vocations when Jack's heart missed a beat. He heard the sound of a vehicle coming along his well-concealed track. Not quite well enough as it turned out.

After a minute, Jack heard a door slam and presently, over the river bank, appeared a visitor.

'What are you up to?' the bloke asked Jack.

'Nothing much. Yourself?'

'Just poking about. What's the fishing like?'

Jack said, 'Dunno. You'll have to ask the pelicans.'

The visitor seemed to be considering something before he asked, 'What's that dog up to?'

Jack looked puzzled. 'Dunno that either. Never seen him before. Just interested to see what he's up to myself. Seems to be towing something, doesn't he? Looks like a net.'

The bloke pulled out his notebook and said, 'Do you know who I am?'

'Nope.'

'I'm the fishing inspector.'

'Thank God for that,' Jack said, 'for a moment there I thought you were the bastard who owned that net and the dog.'

———

Blowing in the wind

'Beans means Heinz', so goes the advertisement. 'Beans means fartz' goes the graffiti. Jack should have featured on the billboards. He was their man and they missed the chance. He was addicted to beans and paid the price, or at least those around him did. No two ways about it.

'No more, Jonathan, my boy; never again. No more beans. I cannot abide the offensive odour after your partaking thereof.'

'What?'

'I can't stand your stink,' his wife Margie stated.

Marriages had foundered because of beans, and Margie had considered joining the throng massing at rallies to demand a worldwide ban. But as a starting point baked beans were outlawed from her household.

Under no circumstances would they or their conse-
quences be tolerated. Heinz had a case to answer.

Still, Jack had to have his beans, at whatever cost.
On the same day as Margie disposed of the last can, Jack
devised a new plan. Right, he thought, to all intents and
purposes, I'll go on a health kick.

'Margie, sweetheart, from now on I'll walk home
from work. It'll do me good. I feel I need the exercise.
After all it's only three kilometres.'

'Great idea,' she said with a smile.

Good, he thought, *I'll call into the café downstairs
at work and have a plateful of beans just after I knock
off. Then, by the time I've walked home, all of the after
effects should have gone. Just for good measure I'll take
the long way home.*

Foolproof. Worked a treat, until . . .

'Darling, did you think I forgot your birthday this
morning?' Margie asked via the phone.

'Er . . .'

'Well, I didn't. Hurry home tonight. It'll be worth
your while, I promise. I know you'll absolutely love it.'

Now Jack got to thinking. Visions of a romantic
dinner for two and the fantasy of Margie wearing not
much at all floated before his eyes. *But first*, he thought,
I've just got to have my beans. No room for compromise

there. But he'd take the short way home and hope the blowout was complete by the time he walked up the steps. The long way was only ever a buffer anyway. He should come in right on time.

That evening, mission completed, he was met by Margie at the front door.

'Darling, I'm going to blindfold you and sit you down at the dining-room table. Hope you don't guess anything.'

Bet it's seafood crepes and custard meringue pie, Jack thought. Yum!

'No peeking. I'm just going to the kitchen for a moment. Be patient. You'll be pleased you were.'

As he sat waiting, to Jack's horror he felt his stomach rumble and growl. Lifting one bum cheek off the chair he had no option but to let go a string of farts of varying pitch, intensity, and audio and cubic capacity. 'Jesus Christ,' he said not so quietly to himself, 'fart like a draught horse on green oats.' He waved his arms about dispersing the stench and was just settling when he was again caught short, this time it was even more pungent and noisy. Thank God he could still hear Margie in the kitchen. 'Fuckin' hell,' he said quietly, 'I'll be lucky to get away with this.' He gave the rotten-egg gas the windmill treatment as fast as he could.

'You're not peeking are you? Won't be a moment.'

'Small mercy,' he spoke aloud as he let another one rip.

'What's that, darling? Did you say something?'

'No. Take your time, sweetheart.'

A short while later he sensed her near presence and caught a whiff of her perfume.

'Just a sec. I'll be back,' she said, touching him lightly on the arm. And then she was off again.

As he heard the pantry door open he said, not so quietly, 'Can't wait to get you in bed later, you little tiger.'

Another fart escaped. Oops! It didn't seem serious but even so he stood up and shook out each trouser leg in turn.

Then she was back.

'Okay, ready now. Happy fiftieth, darling! Surprise!' And she whipped off the blindfold to reveal six of Jack's old school mates and their wives seated at the table.

———

Murphy and the donuts

From a good way off, Pat spotted Murphy entering the bakery. Pat's mate was well-known as a donut addict.

So, with his guts rumbling at the thought of food and not a coin in his pocket, Pat knew immediately what he had to do.

After emerging from the shop, Murphy became aware of Patrick looming near the corner and quickened his pace, but to no avail.

As Pat drew level, breathless, he said, 'Murphy, my old friend, good day to you and a fine one at that.'

'It is, no doubt. And where might ye be heading?'

'Not far at all. In fact, nowhere at all. Just be walking in the sunshine.'

'And sniffing pastries and donuts on the breeze?'

'Now that you mention it, I am a little peckish.'

Murphy thought he'd string him along a bit. 'Ye should be buying something to eat, to be sure.'

'Well, I've not a shilling.'

'Spent it all on the pint, no doubt.'

'Well, no. Not all. I did have a small wager but the donkey ran like one and that made me want to drown me sorrows. I'm a sorry man. Do you think that if I guess how many donuts you have in that bag, you might let me have one?'

Capitulating to his boozy mate's request, Murphy held out the bag and replied, 'Patrick, if you can guess how many are in the bag you can have both of them.'

And Pat said, 'Four.'

———

Meet in the middle

Troy was fair crapping himself (so to speak) with the thought of his forthcoming colonoscopy.

'Eye of a needle sort of stuff, mate,' one friend said.

'Four hours on the dunny beforehand,' said another.

'Have to drink a couple of gallons of vile jungle juice,' said yet another.

'Radar camera up the bum. Pleased it's you and not me,' his brother commented.

But that wasn't all. His doctor decided to perform an endoscopy down Troy's throat the same time. Shit, Troy thought, but then thrift surfaced – save on anaesthetic, hospital stays, inconvenience, save on . . . just save!

As reality set in, and some details of the procedure were outlined, Troy packed a small overnight bag in readiness. On the morning of the appointment he went off to his date with destiny. As a farewell, his sibling hadn't helped the situation when he added, 'I reckon the cameras will meet in the middle and you'll look like a pig on a spit – gear down your neck and up your bum at the same time.'

Time passed. Admission forms, nurses in sassy

uniforms, doctor in green camouflage outfit, needle in the arm – then, oblivion.

As mothers do all across the world, and probably everywhere else too, Troy's sat outside the recovery ward and waited for news.

As nurses drifted by, Troy's mum tried to catch the eye of each as they passed. Finally a nurse approached her.

'I guess you are Troy's mum,' she said.

'Yes, I am. Is he all right?'

'He'll be fine. The doctor will see you in a moment.'

'Thank goodness for that. How's he feeling?'

'Okay. But he seems to have a fixation with food. Looking forward to a meal, I would say. Ever since the anaesthetic started to wear off he's been yelling out something about roast pork done on a spit. He must have worked up quite an appetite.'

———

Fur, Feathers and Fun

'The Kookaburra family must have gone on holidays – they've got their answering machine on.'

Gold fever

Back in the 1890s, Sam and George were making their way to Alaska, to search for gold. It'd taken many months of travel, but they'd almost reached their destination – which was bloody lucky because the amount of tucker they had left in the saddlebags wouldn't have fed an anorexic ant, not for long anyway. As for Sam's brother, Billy, well, he didn't know which way was up, and all he had to do was mush the huskies throughout the day and half the night . . . then cook tea, feed the dogs, wash up and take out the rubbish.

They were setting up at the big mining camp when a loud voice hollered a warning through the birch briars. Translated into Aussie it said, 'All right, you bastards, get this into your thick scones this minute. You can't just rock in here right under our noses and take over.'

That had been their welcome.

'Actually, it'd be better if you mushed off right now. What do you think about that?' the voice continued.

Sam mustn't have thought much of it because right off he marched into the bushes and kneed the loud-mouth, Big Red, in the nuts, and for good measure belted him fair on the lug as Red was doubled over.

While Sam was gloating over Big Red, some clown sneaked up behind with a shovel and cracked him a beauty on top of his beaver cap. All this while, George was getting the arse flogged off him and not putting on much of a show at all. Useless bugger. As for Billy, well, he was cacking himself laughing so hard that no one regarded him as any threat at all, and one of the miners pushed him over into the creek.

'Hmm,' said Sam, when he came to. 'Not good.'

George said something similar a minute later, and Billy stayed down the creek, trying to catch salmon fingerlings in his hat.

Somewhat pale and quiet, Big Red got up and hobbled about a bit, trying not to look pained. When the dust had settled and tempers calmed, one of the other miners, named Hagar, took the lead.

'Look, fellas, no offence meant, but when each of us got here, before we were allowed to stay, we had to pass an initiation.'

'And what would that be?' Sam asked, rubbing the top of his head.

'Well, in the first instance, you will be required to skol a full bottle of Kentucky bourbon without stopping to draw breath.'

'Good as done,' Sam replied without hesitation.

He looked to George.

'No worries, mate,' George answered, feeling his jaw with one hand and fingering the top of his ear with the other.

'Where's Billy?'

'Over there, counting fingerlings,' Big Red said, not game to laugh.

'What else is there to this initiation?' asked Sam.

'You'll have to wrestle a grizzly.'

'Easy,' Sam said. 'Done a bit of that when I was a boy with Davy Crockett.'

'Piece of piss,' George added. 'Saw a doco on it once. Do it on my ear, sort of.'

And Billy called out, 'Fourteen!'

Big Red turned the other way.

'That all?' Sam asked Hagar.

'No. To top it off you'll have to find a dusky maiden and ask her nicely to have sex with you.'

'Interesting,' Sam said.

George agreed. 'Now, run through it again.'

'Right,' Hagar said, 'one. Skol a bottle of whisky. Got that?'

'Yep.'

'Two. Wrestle a grizzly.'

'Gotcha.'

'Three. Sex with a dusky maiden.'

'Sounds good.'

Billy chimed in with, 'What did you say?'

Sam showed the way by polishing off the grog in three glugging gulps, then he wiped his mouth with the back of his hand and said, 'I'll be off then.'

George was a little less of a pig and took six slugs to drain his bottle, burped, farted twice, burped again and said, 'I'll go this way.'

Billy tried to be a big man like Sam and gulped down half the bourbon . . . then passed out. Two hours later he got up, asked what day it was, remembered the initiation challenge and said, 'Shit, which way did the others go?'

Sam was first to step back out of the fir forest the next morning. He looked okay – a bit scratched about, superficial like. No problem.

'I'm going over to the canteen for a venison pie and peas,' he said.

Soon after, George came in, looking a bit buggered, limping slightly, a bit of blood here and there but otherwise sound. Pretty good considering. Mission accomplished.

'Where's Sam? Just want to compare notes.'

Late that afternoon poor bloody Billy crawled in

torn to shreds, pale from the loss of blood, and collapsed at Sam's feet. 'Nearly got it nailed,' he rasped. 'Now, where's the dusky maiden I'm supposed to wrestle?'

———

Herd improver

Barney had a dilemma on his hands. He'd bought a new bull for his dairy herd and it looked like the animal had problems. The herd improver had cost $10000 – a stud bull, he was. Impeccable bloodlines, great conformation, macho looks and balls the size of beer bottles – tallies not stubbies.

Recorded on the registration papers was the bull's name: Tiny Tim. Interesting.

As it turned out, Timmy wouldn't look at a heifer, not even a doe-eyed Jersey. Barney had almost got to the stage of contacting the stud where Timmy was reared, but he decided to give the vet a call first.

'Barney,' said the vet, 'there might be a problem here, but on the other hand Timmy might simply be a shy breeder. Some bulls will only mate in the dark, you know. Take note and come back if you don't notice him doing the do.'

Sleepless night after sleepless night for Barney. No go. The heifers weren't getting in calf. Off to the vet Barney returned to report the lack of progress.

'Oh, well,' the vet said, 'plan B. I'll give you some pills for the bull and we'll see how he reacts to them. Results from this drug have been variable. I won't charge you for them.'

Holy mackerel! Timmy mated with every cow in the herd whether she liked it not. He sneaked up on Barney's wall-eyed saddle horse on her blind side and zapped her. He jumped the fence and went at 200 beef breeders in a paddock nearby. The sex-mad bull got into the local feedlot and fixed up all the females and quite a few steers and bullocks.

Fred, a farmer mate of Barney's from twenty kilometres away, heard about Timmy. Barney got a call from him.

'Barney, how're going? I see you've made the newspapers with your bull. Must be a wonder drug, eh? I don't suppose you've got a few pills left for me to give my poor old worn-out bull to save me buying a new one till next season?'

'No, mate. All gone. Sorry.'

'No worry. I'll call at the vet's and pick some up. What are they called?'

'Can't rightly remember. I threw the box out,' Barney informed him, 'but they're blue, and they taste like peppermint.'

Desert dogs

Three dogs – a blue heeler, a kelpie and an Irish setter – were hitching a ride through the desert on a semitrailer on their way down to the Brisbane Royal for the dog show. When the semi hit a pothole the size of half a bus, they fell off.

The setter started carrying on something fierce, shit-scared, yelping his guts out, and Bluey got the shits with him.

'For God's sake, Irish; it's not the end of the world. We've got a bit of time up our sleeves. I know my way around the bush. We'll be right: just stick with me.'

Irish's fears were momentarily allayed, but it wasn't long before he started up again. Kelpie told him not to be a gutless bastard, and that he'd be okay, so he should quit bellyaching. So what if he had to forfeit his nomination money. Kelpie also knew the desert like the back of his paw, so they'd be right.

So Irish and the others took off to walk back to

civilisation. From time to time they lost sight of each other but always kept within barking distance.

It was during one of these separations that disaster struck. A dogger had been setting traps, and simultaneously they each got caught by their legs.

Predictably, the setter put on a tantrum but the other two remained calm.

'Jesus, mate,' Bluey called to Kelpie, 'The shit's hit the fan over here: I'm caught in a dingo trap.'

Kelpie answered, 'Buggerin' hell, as it happens, me too. What about you, Irish?'

'Yeah, I'm fucked. That's it. All over, red rover. Pull down the curtain.'

Well, Bluey and Kelpie, both being part dingo, had a bit of a yarn over the sand hill, and Bluey told his mate that he'd heard of dingoes chewing their legs off when in similar predicaments.

'Bit radical, mate,' Kelpie said.

'Better than being dead,' Blue answered.

The pair decided to adopt the course of action, and informed Irish who, through a lot of blubbering, took in the news. He had no alternative: he would never again point to a bevy of quail without falling on his guts, but that was still better than being stuck there forever, or when the dogger comes back, whichever's first. So all three began to gnaw their legs off. Blue had his off first, having the highest percentage of dingo blood in him.

'How are you going over there, Kelpie, old mate?'

'Yeah, bit of an ordeal but I'm getting there. Be through soon. What about you, Irish? Getting the hang of it? Bit painful but better than the alternative, eh?'

'Bullshit. Can't make head or tail of your plan. Didn't like the half-arsed idea from the start. I've chewed through three legs and I'm still stuck in this feckin' thing.'

Bobby the horse

All was well on Saturday morning until . . .

'Dad, can I get a pony?'

'No.'

'Dad, you didn't even think about it.'

'I didn't have to.'

So, into the laundry she went.

'Mum, can I get a horse like Amanda's? She goes to pony club on the weekend and wears jodhpurs. Pretty cool, huh?'

'It sounds good, sweetheart, but horses cost a lot and need saddles and floats and things. Go and talk to your father about it.'

Fathers and daughters generally have something special going for them, and Dad's little fingers were twisted and bent from previous encounters.

So, come Monday:

'Mate, the daughter wants a horse. You know all about them, don't you? What do I have to do? Where do I start?'

'Go no further, old buddy. I'm your man. I've got just the pony for you. The son has grown out of it.'

'Sounds good. Tell me about it, a lesson of the equine persuasion, perhaps. Remember, I'm horse illiterate.'

'Well, this little goer is bombproof. No vices at all. Easy to shoe, sweet-tempered, won prizes, you name it. Bobby's only middle-aged, good legs, easy to catch – comes to a call. All you could wish for in a kid's pony.'

Done deal.

Following Monday morning.

'You bastard! That bloody horse you sold me is only good for greyhound tucker. He's got one walleye. He has three good legs but the other one probably got busted kicking the eye out of a needle. He's a hundred years old, and bite – talk about bite – he took a chunk out of the kid's arse as she was getting aboard. That was after we caught the yang. And try and shoe the mongrel? The farrier charged double and said he won't be coming back. Talk about getting taken down.'

'Bloody hell, pal. No need to get nasty. If I was you, I wouldn't be talking too loudly about Bobby like that . . . you'll never get rid of him.'

———————

Nothing to crow about

Ever since the day Mark, the elder in a nestling brood of two, was born, or rather ever since the day he was hatched, he'd been a smartarse. When mum brought home fat worms for dinner, Mark got most of them. He won the state-wide cutest baby competition ~~hands~~ wings down, and secured a contract with an advertising agency to become the face of Edgell. His first commission was with Birds Eye frozen peas, but the company was bought out by McCain so the whole thing fell over.

Regrouping after that setback, Mark concentrated on preening his growing feathers. As vanity took hold, he'd look at every reflective surface he could find – car hubcaps, shop fronts, even the water in the horse trough and the dog's dish. 'Just look at me now,' he'd crow to anyone within his territory.

He went down to the airport to start flying lessons

even before his tail feathers had properly grown, doing the theory first and planning to do the prac later. Mark accomplished that feat before his brother was out of nappies, or to be more accurate, downy 'pull-ups'.

During his adolescence Mark learned to ark louder than his peers. When he practised his arks, he'd experiment with variations until one day his old man slapped him across the beak with his wing. 'That'll get you into farkin' trouble before you're much older, son.'

His little brother, named Cark (because he nearly did when Mark pushed him out of the nest), was only half the size of his big bro, but he kept on keeping on, plugging away steadfastly. His coat was always a bit raggedy. His tail had grown somewhat askew. His eyes were dull and he didn't have much in the way of brains. But he kept soldiering on, rain, hail or shine.

Cark never had quite enough to eat, but at least he had something. Even if he had to eat dingo crap instead of juicy worms, well, that was okay with a bit of Worcestershire sauce over it.

Mark came home stuffed full of food every day, and Cark wondered where he went but was too afraid to follow him to find out. Mark told him he flew to a land of plenty but that only the bravest and strongest birds could manage to get there. In actual fact, Mark was visiting a feedlot where they grain fed cattle barely 3 kilometres away, as the crow flies that is, and spent his days filling up on waste grain in the manure pile.

Every morning before Mark went off over the hill to gorge on his tucker of bull excrement, he'd sit on the fence and *ark* his guts out. This annoyed the crap out of Cark, who hated show-offs. Every evening when Mark came home he'd do the same. This annoyed Cark even more.

But life went on.

Mark got bigger and fatter and glossier from his forays to the feedlot. His world couldn't have been better. His voice had broken and was developing a masculine timbre. The girl crows, flockies not groupies, abounded on all sides. Some days he was plum-tuckered out just seeing to a couple of dozen, but, hell, what a life.

In due course he got to thinking about Cark. *Poor bugger. Maybe I should share my good fortune and gourmet tucker? After all, we are brothers.*

'Cark, buddy, why don't you come with me some days? Over the hill thereaways lies yonder feedlot. Don't you see how happy I am to go off in the mornings. Come with me, brother.'

'Excuse my ignorance, but what's a feedlot?'

'Tell you what, you won't believe your eyes. There are 20000 cattle over there in big pens. All they do is eat, so there is plenty of leftover food everywhere, but there's a catch: the waste grain is embedded in their shit. Still, there's a lot of goodness in it. Just look at me. And the worms! You won't believe the worms! But, once again, they are under all the shit.'

'Dunno, bro. I'm happy enough here. Life is okay.'

'Suit yourself, loser.'

Next day he tried again with his brother but to no avail. So he *arked* his guts out, boasting again about his accomplishments, brains and good looks. Now this was really starting to get fair on Cark's goat. Every day Mark hammered him with the same old story.

Sitting on the fence post one Thursday morning not far from their roosting tree, Mark was at poor old Cark again. 'Just over yonder hill, bro. follow me. I'm the smartest bird ever hatched.'

Blam! And there lay Mark, dead at Cark's feet with his guts blown out, and farmer Joe holding the smoking shotgun.

Moral of the story? If you're full of bullshit, it pays to keep your mouth shut.

———

Teepee

'So good to see you, Spotted Fawn. How is school going?'

'Father, I'm in third-year uni.'

Chief Sitting Bull straightened his wing feathers, and said apologetically, 'Sorry, sweetheart, I forgot. What are you studying again?'

'Native American studies. Here is your birthday present. Hope you like it. I must go and catch up with mother. Bye.'

'Tell your sister I'd like to see her, sweetheart.'

'I will, Father. See you soon.' Spotted Fawn leant down and kissed him.

'Floating Cloud, my how you've grown. Your mother said you could be a model if you wanted to. And she's right: you're beautiful. You'll turn the heads of many braves. What are you doing again?' Sitting Bull asked, acutely aware that he'd stuffed up with Spotted Fawn.

'Pa, if I've told you once I've told you a hundred times: I've got a hairdressing apprenticeship. Now, if you don't mind I've got to go. I forgot it was your birthday. Sorry.'

Nothing changed there, he thought, spoilt brat.

'Raging River, how goes it, son? I hear you've passed your first initiation with flying colours. Now all you've got to do is pull down a bison, eh? I put my first head-lock on one when I was twelve, so you've got a hard act to follow. You've got something to aspire to. My record still stands.'

'Yes, Dad, they all tell me you were the greatest brave this tribe has ever produced. I'm proud of you, but I reckon I can knock you off your perch anytime I want to. You seem to brag a lot.'

'Yes, young man, I'm sure you could do me in right this moment if you chose, but as for your inheritance of four teepees and six tomahawks, well, that of course could be another thing.'

As Raging River made a quick exit, smarting as he went, his father called to his back, 'Ask your young sister to come and see me. Tell her I've got a little something for her.'

Sitting Bull thought he might have heard the word 'Bastard' on the breeze, but he couldn't be sure. Years of listening to bellowing buffaloes had half stuffed his ears. In came Spring Flower at a trot. She was his unstated favourite of the brood. She was a beautiful, sweet-natured child, who got special treatment even if she was a bit slow at school. As a saving grace, she could stitch up a pair of moccasins before church on Sunday morning. She was quickly becoming the boot maker of the tribe. Not exactly a feminine trade but bloody useful.

'Dad, Raging River said you've got something for me.'

'Oh, yes, I nearly forgot,' he said, fumbling under his poncho. 'I've been saving it for you. Here you are, darling,' he said, handing her a Picnic bar.

'Thanks! How did you know they were my very favourite?'

'Fathers know these things. I saw a telly advert for them a while ago.'

'Pleased you did, Dad.'

He smiled fondly at her and said, 'I'll have to get ready to go to the powwow soon, precious. When you go, would you ask your little brother to come in for a brief call?'

'Okay, bye.' She gave him a big hug and sweet kiss.

'Hello, son,' Sitting Bull greeted his delicate youngest son, and realised he had a bloody big job in front of him making a brave out of the lad.

'Hello, Daddy. Do you know what I've been doing?'

'No.' Sitting Bull shuddered.

'Plaiting mummy's hair.'

Shit, Sitting Bull thought, the job's just got bigger.

'Daddy, there's been something I've wanted to ask you for a long time now.'

'Fire away, my son,' Sitting Bull said and wondered why the hell he spoke like that.

'Well, my brother and sisters have cool names like "Raging River", "Floating Cloud", "Spring Flower" and "Spotted Fawn". They sound like proper tribal names. What about me? How did I get my name?'

'Son, it is tradition. On the day you were each born, the first thing I saw outside the tepee doorway, well, that became your name. Why do you ask, Two Dogs F---ing?'

Childproof

One and a half metres tall and childproof – a bit like me, Billy's mum reckoned. With a kid like Billy you had to be. But she was actually referring to the fence that was to be erected around their new swimming pool. The council by-law decreed that swimming pool fences should be 1.5 metres tall and constructed of such and such material, by this or that method, and by workmen who held university degrees. The pool fence should be childproof and fitted with a $2000 gate that had a lock nobody could reach, let alone Billy's mum.

But all that hadn't come into play yet because although the swimming pool was completed and full of water, there was no fence around it at all. However, Billy's dad was forced to address the fencing issue when a cow drowned in the pool, and he busted quite a few tiles with the tractor trying to snig it out.

As usual, tradesmen were scarce and charged exorbitant prices, and until Billy's dad could find a suitable contractor he'd erect a single 240-volt electric wire around the pool.

When Billy's mum protested that a metre-high electric fence wouldn't keep Billy from drowning, his father said, 'Bugger Billy, he can swim like a fish. I don't want to lose another cow.'

For the moment the knock-up, gap-fill measure seemed to have the desired effect.

It could be construed by those who knew him and those who'd heard of him that Billy was a cheeky shit of a kid. He annoyed the bejesus out of his bigger sisters. From time to time they got properly fed up with him. The little turd needed regular comeuppance, and the newly erected electric fence provided a great opportunity to put Billy in his place.

The heartless sisters had devised a readjustment for him, whereby one would stand by the piss-weak electric fence, and by holding the wire, demonstrate without adverse reaction that it held no current. Then she would implore Billy not to be a wuss and to have a go. Meanwhile the other would hide in the shed and switch on the unit when Billy's hand touched it. If he was a bastard, they were worse.

But Billy was a smart little bugger. One dewy early morning he decided to show up his siblings. After having been caught once, he had it figured. Knowing that the hot wire was active, he donned his gumboots, dragged a concrete block to the fence, hopped up on it and called to the sisters, 'Nur, nur, na, nur nur.'

Sensing fun, the dog bounded over to Billy, licked his hand and completing the circuit via its tongue shorted them both to the wet grass.

It was said that Billy never went near the wire again. It was also said that the dog never went near Billy again either.

———

Hercules

The conversation in the bar of the Imperial had ebbed and flowed for a couple of hours. It was Saturday afternoon and Pete, Bernie and Cracker (so named because he wore his shorts too low) had covered the usual topics of conversation. While the trio yarned, Cracker's chihuahua had sat under a bar stool and dozed off. Bernie's blue heeler had caused and won three fights, and Pete's kelpie had yarded two hundred sheep into the pub parking yard.

Firstly, of course, the weather was discussed. Same old shit. Then there was the tennis. Not much interest. Football – bit of an argument. But then came an improbable boast from Bernie.

'Yeah, I reckon I've got the toughest dog around.'

That pricked up the ears.

'Yeah, that blue heeler of mine is so tough he once fought three pit bulls in succession and beat them all.'

'Bullshit,' Cracker said.

'Yeah, it is bullshit because not only did he beat up the three pit bulls in the first instance, they put two more 'bulls in at once to try and get the better of him, but no go. Nup. He grabbed one by the throat and while he was shaking the life out of it, he fended off the other with a back leg. Seeing what was happening to its mate, the second dog lay on the ground and whimpered. Blue just took one look at the gutless wonder, pissed on him, jumped the enclosure and mated with a poodle that was watching the spectacle. Talk about tough.'

'Some dog,' Pete said, 'but that's nothing. He's just a thug. Obviously he's got nothing between the ears.'

That seemed to dampen the conversation somewhat for a quarter of an hour.

'Well, what's so special about your kelpie?' Bernie said, recovering from the slight. 'Looks like all it can do is round up a few sheep. I've seen hundreds of dogs do that. Pretty ordinary, if you ask me.'

'Round up a few sheep?! For God's sake, Bernie, this dog once drove 5400 ewes and 4126 lambs across the Nullarbor . . . in a week . . . on his own . . . without a bite to eat. I reckon that'd take some beating.'

Cracker had been quiet ignoring the chihuahua at his feet, no doubt obviously embarrassed by the useless rat of a thing he called a dog.

Bernie gave Pete a wink as he addressed Cracker. 'Mate, I need a leak. When I come back, you can fill me in on your hound's expertise?' And then he laughed.

While Bernie was away describing figure eights on the urinal wall, Cracker said to Pete, 'My little fellow does karate. Watch this.'

He leant down and said quietly to the chihuahua, 'Come on, little mate, show Pete what you're made of. Karate that bar stool.'

The little bloke took up a karate stance, yipped, 'Heeyah!' and demolished the bar stool in six seconds flat. It lay in splintered ruins.

A couple of minutes later, after the barman had cleaned up the mess, Bernie appeared in the doorway and said, 'Okay, Cracker, what's your excuse for a dog's claim to fame?'

Pete interjected. 'Bern, my friend, Cracker's hound does karate – black belt. You should see him go.'

Disbelievingly, Bernie said, 'Karate, my arse . . . *aarrrggghhh!*'

———

*'Oh no! I heard BaBa
was going to get the chop.'*

Across the Board

*'Seems it wasn't such a good idea
using the crop duster for the
Anzac Day fly over after all.'*

HRH Prince Charles Duke of Cornwall

Western Queensland has a few claims to fame. Two of them are world icons. One, the airline Qantas, was founded in Winton – way out to buggery – back in the 1920s, and the other, the Australian Stockman's Hall of Fame, at Longreach, was opened to the public in 1988.

God knows who was at the 1920s launch, but there was a bloody huge crowd at the Hall of Fame turnout. The speeches went on and on. The founding fathers, Hugh Sawrey and R. M. Williams, received accolades that resounded across the country, and further.

As is protocol in the dominions, a member of the royal family had been approached to conduct the opening ceremony. On the flip of a twenty-cent coin – heads the Queen, tails the Duke of Cornwall – it was the platypus.

'Well, looks like you're it, Chas,' the mayor had said, making a note on his wrist.

At Longreach airport Charles got out of a twin-engine Cessna, which had been seconded because his highness's personal jumbo had let them down, collapsing a universal joint and shearing off a tail shaft. From a distance, the delegation of dignitaries who'd arranged to meet him was surprised at his choice of dress. He was wearing a beige polyester short-sleeved, short-legged safari suit last seen in the early seventies. His footwear consisted of a pair of brown-leather sandals with barely detectable white socks that reached almost to his knees. To top it all off, he wore a snug-fitting Davy Crockett–style hat made from silver fox skin with the fox's tail hanging down his back.

As Charlie stepped onto the tarmac, sealed with goat-shit gravel, the blast of hot air from the props blew off his head gear and flapped up his comb-over. Not a good start.

In due course, following the official welcome, they headed off to the grog tent. After Charles had declined a pint of Newcastle Brown Pilsener, one of the officials, in fact the deputy mayor, was heard to ask the prince something quietly over a glass of orange juice.

'Jeez, Charlie, what made you wear that get-up, old boy?'

'Say what? Is there something wrong with my suit?' Charles replied in a brow-wrinkled manner. Looking down, he quickly brushed off a patch of red dust from his shoulder, so he could use the same hand to stir the flies around his face.

The deputy mayor responded, 'No, Charlie, old son, it's quite all right. Safari suits, particularly the drip-dry, wrinkle-free ones, are perfect attire for the tropics. Some of our own still wear them if the occasion is really formal.'

'Well, what then? Is it my sandals and socks? I have worn them for as long as I can remember. Am I out of fashion, would you say?' Charles was getting really concerned.

'No, they're okay, Chas. There're a few Poms about here who still cling to that custom. We're quite used to them. It's that bloody fox hat, mate. Whatever made you wear that sort of headdress here in the outback?'

'Actually, Mummy told me to wear it,' Charles replied. 'I was having a shower at Buckingham Palace, and as I dried off and put on my deodorant, which, I might add, I had a lot of trouble finding, I called out, "Mummy, I'm planning to wear my safari suit. Shall I wear the pith helmet I wore on my trip to Africa?"

'She answered, "Where are you going, son?"

'"Longreach, Queensland," I told her.

'After a moment or two she answered, "Where the fock's 'at?"

'So I did.'

———

Promises, promises

The campaign was long and hard. Right at the outset Tony was left in the starting blocks when the media became focused on the issue of his budgie smugglers. He said later that his budgie had become caught between a rock and a hard place and when he looked up, Julia was a couple of noses out in front.

As time went on, there was a slight swing back to the Libs. Somehow, the recent stabbing of Kevin had hit the newspapers again. It's not Australian, the public said, not the Australian way. For God's sake, the man could speak to mandarins, how good is that? Surely he deserved better treatment. Bugger Labor, even stalwarts said.

However, even though the newspapers were giving Tony plenty of good press, his photos lacked the ability to make his face a familiar image. According to reliable sources, most women focused on his other attributes. Most men fell about pointing and laughing.

Julia on the other hand was everywhere, kissing babies and spreading germs. Not being totally at ease with little mites slobbering down the front of her smock and coughing in their rompers, she dropped a couple (of babies, that is) and lost some ground as a result.

Not to be outdone, Tony shook hands with anyone and everyone (even a mannequin in Myer) until he got RSI in his right hand. Problem. Doing things left handed felt a bit foreign but he got the hang of it. He soon had things in hand, so to speak . . . but not long later he ended up with tennis elbow. Even so, he had to act fast to maintain momentum.

Fortunately he had left his trump card till last. He'd had his ears to the ground, for a change. The oldies. Nursing homes. Good, thinking people who had time on their hands to consider things properly and make rational judgements.

Pumped up with his own good idea and the clever way he'd kept it in the bag for so long, much akin to his budgie, he was fair bursting with anticipation at his impending coup. He knew that if he could make whirl-wind appearances at nursing homes across the country he could come from behind and pip Julia at the post – no mean feat, as it necessitated overtaking Julia and a couple seconds later, her nose as well.

Brimming with confidence, Tony trotted off to the local TriCare facility.

As he approached the nearest old dear in the lounge, he was heard to say, 'Hello. If I am elected, I will be your new prime minister.'

'What's that? You'll have to speak up. Help me with this blasted hearing aid.'

'Do you know who I am?'

To which she replied, 'No, dear, but if you ask at the front desk, they will be able to tell you.'

———

Luigi the Great

'Luigi, how come you're living up here on your own? How long have you been here? Whatever has happened? You were once a great man.'

'I, too, know this. It is not my choice to live like a hermit on this mountain. I was once the Mayor of Athens. I built the new Acropolis and I was the toast of Greece, and now they've banished me,' he sobbed.

'Why so?'

'I built the new town hall and all the roads that lead to it.'

It was easy to see the great man was gutted. He might as well have been a lonely shepherd.

'There must have been a reason for your fall from grace.'

'I introduced a new system of taxation to the benefit of all. It was very popular; every worker was better off because of my sweeping reforms.'

It was a pitiful sight: this old man living out his twilight years alone in exile.

'I won every election unopposed. I had the highest popularity rating of any leader in the history of the nation.'

Luigi seemed angry but resigned to his fate just the same.

'What can the reason be if all you say is true? It seems so sad.'

'Yes, my friend, it is. All lost for just one little goat . . .'

———

Four-leaf dive charters

Finnegan and Dermot had come a long way from the freezing fishing grounds of the North Sea. No more rolling seas and breakers over the bow, no more chattering teeth and red noses. No siree. Not anymore.

It was glorious weather when the pair arrived in Cairns, looking for adventure and a business opportunity. The tourist season usually ran from 1 January to 31 December so this seemed the place to be. Quickly they perceived there was a gap in the market for another professional dive-boat charter business.

Knowing that Dermot was the brains of the outfit, Finnegan asked, 'Dermie, me mate, what sort of boat will we buy? Would a four-metre tinny be big enough or would it be overkill?'

Dermot roared laughing to the extent that he risked insulting his mate. 'Begorrah and all, don't you know anything, me dim-witted mate? We'll need at least a five-metre model,' Dermot announced, 'and at least a thirty-horsepower outboard.'

Finnegan's eyes showed he was impressed. His escalating excitement at becoming an entrepreneur could barely be concealed.

'How big an esky would we need, Derm?'

'No, me mate, we won't need refrigeration. Irish Cream Whisky can be drunk at room temperature, and we'll only need half a dozen bottles a day. We'll allow a bottle per customer so we won't have storage problems as a result.' Then he added, tapping his forehead, 'Up here for dancing,' then pointing to his feet, 'down there for thinking.'

Finnegan frowned and looked thoughtful, repeating Dermot's actions.

Dermot went on. 'I'll be supposing that the story you told me about being a Navy Frogman in the war was the whole truth and nought but it?'

'Well . . .' Finnegan went to say in his defence.

'Well, what?'

'Derm, be reasonable. I saw a movie once and it looked easy – zip up your wet suit, strap on your air tank, stand up on the side of the boat and fall in back-wards.'

'You're a worry, Finnegan. Get down to the library and find a book on scuba diving. We've got four Pommie tourists arriving next week and we want to present as a professional outfit.'

But despite the misgivings, stuff-ups, doubts and a fair bit of frigging-about all was brought to rights on the morning of the maiden voyage. Finnegan and Derm saw fit to celebrate with a bottle of whisky. They were just polishing off the last of it as the Poms arrived on the wharf. In due course the Englishmen boarded.

Even though the equipment was flimsy and decidedly lacking, and the English were initially apprehensive, by halfway through the second bottle of whisky a holiday mood had prevailed.

Using the GPS, Dermot anchored over a coral bombie and the divers kitted up. In sequence the three divers plunged backwards into the water.

Just before the fourth bloke inserted his mouthpiece, he turned to Finnegan and said, 'I've often wondered why all divers jump off backwards.'

Finnegan shook his head at the Englishman's ignorance.

'Begorrah man, if they jumped forwards they'd still be in the boat.'

————

Tax department

The cash economy has always been alive and well. It makes petty criminals out of us all, but lots of families would be worse off if tax had to be paid on every cent earned. Charlie and Edna, an older couple whose children had grown up and left home, and who still ran a small farming enterprise, had been in a running battle with the tax office for years.

'No profit this year, love. We'll show the bastards. For once they won't get any tax out of us. Good thing, the drought. Got to get a positive now and again,' Charlie said to Edna.

'Really positive, eh? No tax and nothing to eat. How do we fix that?'

Charlie had got to thinking these last few months. He had a plan, flimsy as it was.

'I reckon we rationalise the whole farm operation to

create a bit of cash flow. Okay by you, love?'

'Have to be. What have you got in mind?'

'Well, the old header has been written-off in the books for years. Okay, out it goes for cash. Half value but cash. We barely use it anyway. If we trade it in, we'll pay tax on it.'

'We should have been hiring contractors anyway,' Edna said, starting to look hopeful.

'We'll check out the depreciation schedule to see what other savings we can wangle there. There will be other machinery for sure.'

'I'm still listening.'

'And if we say a third of our breeders have died in the drought, we could sell them real cheap for cash.'

After being put into action, the plan was working like the bull in the heifer paddock.

Everything was on track until a letter from the tax department arrived.

'Shit,' Charlie said, as he started to read. 'Looks like we've been audited. Friggin' hell, Edna, look at this, if you can decipher the gobbledegook. '

'It's a random audit by the looks,' she answered.

'Bullshit. You can't trust the bastards. They've had us in their sights for years.'

'Charlie, I think that's called paranoia.'

'Don't know what paranoia means, but I reckon they've got it in for us.'

Edna shook her head, then burst out laughing. 'Don't think so, Charlie boy. Listen to this over the page.

'"It has come to our notice that you have made a false claim in this year's lodgement. We would like to point out that no claims for livestock will be recognised in your depreciation schedule."'

'That's ridiculous. We didn't include any livestock. Didn't even sell them, did we, dear?' He winked at her.

'It's the "artesian bore".' Edna couldn't say anything more as she fought for control. She took off her glasses and wiped her eyes. 'They think artesian bores are livestock.'

Charlie wrote back: 'Pigs might fly in your department but this old tusker's got a windmill sitting on top of him. Claim to stand as is, please.' He nearly added 'dimwit' but thought better of it.

The claim was allowed but the accompanying letter stated in part, 'Even though your claim for depreciation on an artesian bore has been recognised, we ask you to explain why you included depreciation on another item of livestock, namely "hydraulic ram".'

————

Save the planet

The United Nations had brought so much pressure to bear on the prime minister, she eventually acceded and held a summit on climate change. At the meeting the UN Chairman called the Aussies a pack of bastards with little concern for the environment. The prime minister replied that we couldn't have that and swore she'd do something to reverse public opinion.

Three months later the prime minister was ready to tackle this mammoth undertaking, and passed on a memo to the head of the Public Service, saying they should gear up as a directive would be forthcoming. In due course, the directive arrived at the state premier's office for its consideration. The premier's department then produced a ~~white~~ green paper using a hundred thousand tonnes of woodchip.

That done, the outcome was passed on to the department of local government. The recipients were a little lukewarm about climate change, arguing that there was enough climate around anyway so why change it. However, they did as bidden and passed on their opinion to the mayors of the various local councils for their consideration.

The mayor of one particular council was enraptured with the idea of Australia taking a more proactive role in reducing global warming and planned to plant trees up selected streets in his town. To this end he contacted the works supervisor to order some bottlebrush seedlings from the state nursery. As they were fresh out of bottlebrushes, they suggested prickly pear, but after some consideration the idea was rejected because it was thought dogs might injure their willies trying to piddle on them. So the mayor opted to wait for more stock to be grown. That only took eighteen months.

It was a great day when a Hilux ute, half full of seedlings in six-inch pots, arrived at the council. The rejoicing was dampened only a little when, because it was half an hour till knockoff time, the staff of eight refused to unload because the forklift had a flat tyre and they hadn't been able to locate the puncture repair kit all week. But by mid-morning Monday the ute had been unloaded.

One day not long after, from way along the street, a ratepayer observed two council workmen progressing along the nature strip. One bloke was digging holes and the other was following along behind filling them in. *Interesting*, he thought, *what's going on?*

As they progressed nothing further was revealed.

The ratepayer had first thought that the men were trying to locate a cable, but no, it seemed not. Closer and closer they came and the householder became more and more mystified. Finally it got the better of him. When the workmen drew level he simply had to find out what they were doing.

'Well,' said Blue, leaning on his shovel, 'you can see that it's my job to dig the holes for tree planting. And it's Snodger's job to fill them in.' He indicated towards his mate, who was busily shovelling dirt into a half-filled hole. Then he added, 'And it's Pat's job to drop the seedlings in the holes, but he's away sick today.'

————

Baggage handler

Given the opportunity, Wasyl Tasic would more than likely lift up one side of a jumbo jet while three mechanics replaced half a dozen tyres. Wasn't so heavy, he would have said, just a bit awkward. At every turn Wasyl never tired of repaying his perceived debt for his new life in Australia after the war.

'For fuck's sake, Wasyl, slow down, mate. You don't have to run everywhere,' his good mate Action Jackson advised.

Action was so named because one day he might get into action. So far, over the three years he'd been employed as a baggage handler at the airport, no unnecessary movement on his behalf had been detected. Others were less gracious and called him 'Blisters'– he showed up after the work was done. But for some reason Wasyl stuck to him like shit to a blanket.

'Mate,' Action said, 'you'll work the rest of us out of a job. Work to union rules. Ease off.'

'What is union?' Wasyl asked.

'The job you have when you haven't got a job. Clayton's job, mate.'

Wasyl frowned, opened his mouth and looked like he was about to ask about Claytons, but then must have changed his mind because he closed it again.

Twenty or so minutes after smoko, Action had barely pulled up his trousers, zipped his fly, washed his hands, given himself the once over in the mirror and combed his hair before he heard the loud speaker.

'Baggage handler in bay three, please wait for aircraft to come to a halt before approaching.'

Fuck, Action thought, *bloody Wasyl. He'll get me the sack.*

Not to be thwarted, Wasyl had a trailer half loaded before Action arrived.

'Wasyl, you stupid bastard. Wait for me next time.'

Action nearly shat himself with the dark look Wasyl gave him. It spelled hurt, slight, ridicule.

'Why you want me to wait? I know job. No wait. You too slow.'

With suicidal bravado Action continued, trying to ignore his mate's offence.

'Wasyl, you've only been here six minutes and you go so fast nobody gets time to show you how to do things properly.'

Because Wasyl had averted his eyes and made no comment, Action thought that might be the end of it. But it wasn't. In the lunch room things came to a head, and they knew it was coming because Wasyl sat alone, brooding.

Finally he stood and announced angrily, 'You bastards all think I know fuck nothing, but I know fuck all.'

You could have heard a grasshopper burp.

———

Shifting house

Yes, this is my ute and no, I won't help you shift on the weekend.

'Well, I'll be rooted,' Gus said to his mate Davey, looking at the new sign on the back of the headboard of Lionel's Nissan ute, which was parked in his driveway. 'Guess that doesn't apply to me, though, us being close mates an all.'

'How long since you've seen Lionel?' Davey asked.

'A while now.'

'How long is a while?'

'Not since I snotted him at the Christmas party.'

'Hmm,' Davey said.

'He's a good bloke.'

'Hmm. Generally you don't get about snotting your mates.'

'No, guess not. We'd better skedaddle out of here before he sees us. Well, we'll have to figure out a plan B for helping Janey shift on Saturday.'

A decision was made that, as a prudent alternative, an eight by five-metre cage-box trailer on Gus's Commodore might be suitable for the job of relocating his daughter Janey to a fourteenth floor high-rise down at the Gold Coast.

'Here's the place,' Davey exclaimed, reading the Refidex upside down. 'No, sorry. That's Number 96. Looks better the other way round.'

Finally they found the place and parked outside the gated complex.

'We'll have to go into the underground car park to unload,' Gus said.

'Reckon that mattress on top of the trailer will fit under the roller door?' Davey asked, sizing up the opening, 'and how do we get the door up anyway? Looks pretty high tech.'

'It's right. I've got an electronic security thingo. Janey sent it up to me during the week. It only lets reputable people enter.'

'That's us, all right,' his mate said.

Gus swiped the card, and the roller door rose up like clockwork. Then, after a few moments, something seemed to go wrong with it. With the furniture removal outfit only halfway through the opening, the roller door slammed and crashed down half a dozen times in quick succession between the car and the trailer, on the drawbar, and finally stayed there, bent into a half moon.

Gus's fondly voiced opinion of electronics might have been hasty and ill considered, perhaps even crude, maybe downright fuckin' filthy, but so be it.

The site manager who came to their rescue was known to be a lovely natured fellow by all accounts. However that proved to be utter bullshit. But all was resolved amicably by Gus quoting his Visa card number.

With the status quo somewhat restored, Davey suggested, 'We'll take this folding bed up first, eh?'

'Okay. Simple.'

Into the lift they went and set the heavy steel-framed folding bed between them, standing on its edge, facing the door.

Up they went. Floors 10-11-12- etc.

Snap!

On the bed frame, the spring-loaded locking clips, one either side, hadn't been fastened properly. The bed sprung open and, as it was just over two metres long, and the elevator 2.4 metres wide, there were Davey and Gus pinned against either side of the lift and each doubled over from the whack in the nuts.

It took a trip to the top floor and back before they recovered sufficiently to extricate themselves from the predicament.

———————

Irish penfriend

On his first trip to Australia, Sean landed at Sydney Airport on Qantas flight 46 at nine o'clock on Wednesday morning and rang Jack, his penfriend of ten years. The two had corresponded since they were ten-year-olds, continuing to write all throughout adolescence; they were almost like brothers.

'Friggin' hell, Sean,' Jack told him as he took the call at work. 'You're not supposed to be here till nine o'clock Friday night.'

'To be sure, but we picked up a bit of speed after we crossed the equator.'

Jack thought, *How the hell can I keep him entertained till knock-off time?*

Off the top of his head Jack said, 'Sean, get in a taxi – you know my address. The key is under the wheelie bin . . . no, you wanker, *under* it, not in it. Get in your togs and go to Bondi for a swim. Check out the talent for the afternoon. You might even get lucky, if your tan doesn't dazzle them too much. I'll catch you later.'

At half-past five Jack headed home to catch up with his mate, who was sitting on the back steps with his beach towel wrapped around his waist, looking dejected.

'How are you, mate? Why the long face? Wasn't Bondi to your liking?'

'No. There were a lot of beautiful girls there, but they didn't seem to like me.'

Jack stood in front of his mate, looking thoughtful. 'Bugger the women. Want a beer?'

As Sean stood up, his towel slipped to the ground.

'Jesus!' Jack exclaimed. 'No wonder the girls didn't want to know you – look at your togs! Tomorrow you can wear an old pair of my Speedos; the women won't be able to resist.'

Thursday afternoon when Jack arrived home, there was Sean nearly in tears.

'Mate, what could be so bad? Are you homesick?'

'No, the beach girls wouldn't give me a second glance. I'm getting a complex.'

'Okay, take off that towel and let me take another look at you.'

As Sean dropped his towel, Jack shook his head. 'Shit, mate. I can see the trouble: you've got nothing there. Tomorrow when you go down to the surf, jam a spud down the Speedos. That'll get them. Guaranteed.'

Never to be put off, Sean did as he was bidden. He had complete trust in his mate. But the next afternoon, he was inconsolable once again.

'Not only will the girls not hang around,' Sean sniffed, 'they take off like Kilkenny cats with a Doberman after them.'

'Mate, there must be something you're doing wrong,' Jack concluded. 'Here, get that towel off and show me.'

Sean did so.

'You bloody clown, Sean. You were supposed to shove the spud down the *front* of your Speedos.'

————

Friar Tuck

'I'm afraid, Friar, my wayward child, that behaviour such as yours requires punishment, and I must impose a fitting penance. You'll be required to sit on a termite mound in the blazing sun for the entire summer and meditate on your sins. Even then, absolution might still not be given. If it is denied, then sitting on the mound for a further six months in weather that will freeze your balls into marbles could help the matter. That, as I think of it, might not necessarily be a bad thing. Your sins are considerable. It would be a shame to have to report goings-on such as yours to the abbot. Sitting on a rock is commendable, no doubt, but doing more than navel-gazing behind it, well, that's entirely another thing.

Celibacy is God's decree. Forgiveness for masturbation comes at a price.

'Is there an alternative, brother? I doubt I would survive such a trial.'

'Well, now that you mention it, there is a slightly less arduous punishment; it's more of a mental test. We do have a vacancy in the abbey basement, although the appointment would last for twelve months, and you would be required to toil twenty hours a day, seven days a week.'

'Brother, may I ask what my task would be?'

'Transcribing the scriptures, Friar. We need fifty copies by winter solstice. Each year, since 1382, we have had that number transcribed. Two per week should bring you in on time. As you likely know, carbon paper hasn't yet been invented to reduce the workload. Even so, working in sextuplicate would still be a chore of some magnitude, although it is somewhat remiss of me to use such terminology. However, this task also comes at a price. After one year in the dungeon with only a dim candle to light your work, the likelihood is that you will be near blind when you emerge into daylight. It is your choice.'

'May I sit on my rock to meditate on my immediate future?'

'Permission granted, my child; however I suggest that you do not take anything into your own hands during your meditation.'

'No, I shall not make any further habit of it. Indeed, I shall keep my hands right out of my habit.'

Decision reached, within a few hours the friar was ensconced in the dungeon with a heavy heart, the promised candle, a half-loaf of unleavened bread, a water jug, a stack of volumes on his left-hand side and a blank one before him. Near an inkwell lay a few use-less worn-out feather quills.

Jesus Christ, he thought, *how the hell am I going to write with them?* He decided to ask the head monk for some new ones before he got started.

'Friar, don't bother me just now. I'm busy,' said the monk. 'Just help yourself. You should repair to the fowl roost and pluck every cock you can see.'

'I'm begging your pardon?'

'Pluck, you idiot!'

The transcription was monotonous and painstakingly slow work, and the friar had ample time to reflect on his indiscretions as he went. However, the program was interrupted during the Friday afternoon of the first week, just as the friar was about to pen the last paragraph of the first volume. He referred back to an early copy of the scriptures in the monastery bookcase to check the spelling of the word 'cathedral'. But in the line below another word caught his eye. He halted as if struck by the hand of God himself.

Holy jumping Jehoshaphat, upon the head of the Pope, he thought. Surely not. I should check back further. And he did so. Then he checked again . . . and then came the revelation. An ink splat on page 557 had caused the problem, partly obscuring a letter. An apprentice in 1413, not bothering to check details had carelessly transcribed it.

Out into the blinding sunlight the friar ran, after bribing the guard with the rest of his rations. Screaming in delight, he burst into room after room of novices and left a trail of exaltation behind him.

The response from the middle orders, though quieter, was just as excited and caused an eager departure from afternoon prayers. Mutterings akin to 'My goodness, hasn't time flown. I must repair to the cloister to see if I can locate Brother Michael for guidance,' could be heard.

The wise ones, burnt-out old buggers, mostly, collapsed into inconsolable tears as the friar continued to spread the news.

'They got it wrong! They got it wrong! The word was "celebrate"!'

———

'This reclining, vibrating
massaging seat is
so good I feel like
I'm floating on air.'